MW01225490

PENGUIN BOOKS
THE GREAT INDIAN LOVE STORY

Ira Trivedi has lived in nine different cities, across four countries and three continents. She has an MBA from Columbia Business School, New York, and a BA from Wellesley College, Massachusetts. Her first novel was the best-selling *What Would You Do to Save the World?: Confessions of a Could-Have-Been Beauty Queen*.

THE
GREAT
INDIAN
Love Story

IRA TRIVEDI

PENGUIN BOOKS

PENGUIN BOOKS
Published by the Penguin Group
Penguin Books India Pvt. Ltd, 11 Community Centre, Panchsheel Park,
New Delhi 110 017, India
Penguin Group (USA) Inc., 375 Hudson Street, New York, New York 10014,
USA
Penguin Group (Canada), 90 Eglinton Avenue East, Suite 700, Toronto, Ontario,
M4P 2Y3, Canada (a division of Pearson Penguin Canada Inc.)
Penguin Books Ltd, 80 Strand, London WC2R 0RL, England
Penguin, Ireland, 25 St Stephen's Green, Dublin 2, Ireland (a division of Penguin
Books Ltd)
Penguin Group (Australia), 250 Camberwell Road, Camberwell, Victoria 3124,
Australia (a division of Pearson Australia Group Pty Ltd)
Penguin Group (NZ), 67 Apollo Drive, North Shore 0632, New Zealand (a division
of Pearson New Zealand Ltd)
Penguin Group (South Africa) (Pty) Ltd, 24 Sturdee Avenue, Rosebank,
Johannesburg 2196, South Africa

Penguin Books Ltd, Registered Offices: 80 Strand, London WC2R 0RL, England

First published by Penguin Books India 2009
Copyright © Ira Trivedi 2009

10 9 8 7 6 5 4 3 2 1

This is a work of fiction. Names, characters, places and incidents are either the
product of the author's imagination or are used fictitiously, and any resemblance
to any actual person, living or dead, events or locales is entirely coincidental.

ISBN 9780143063889

Typeset in Weiss by Inosoft Systems, Noida
Printed at Thomson Press India Ltd, New Delhi

This book is dedicated to my Balgopal. For His blessings, for showing me the path when there was no light, for giving me faith when I thought I would plummet. I am always in Your service.

For my family—Daddy, Mumma, Misha, Anjani, Anant-Vijay and Vikas. You are my strength and my hope. I am grateful and thankful to God for having you in my life.

For my soul sisters, SP and AO, for being with me every step of the way.

＊

Tumultuous—that is how I feel when I think of him. Warm and fuzzy, hot and cold, all at the same time. I think of his fair face, his hard, piercing eyes and dark hair, his gentle hands that could be rough with impatience, and his crooked smile that made me yearn. There were other things about him that also made me yearn, I think with a smile—his strong, magnificent body that made me go weak. The effect he has on me is wonderful, yet at times it is confusing and terrifying. I think of him when I wake up in the afternoon, and when I fall asleep at dawn. I waited for him to call so I could run to him and be cradled in his arms again. I ached for him all the time because with him I feel special.

＊

Prologue

I met Serena at a point when I was desperately lonely and bored with my life. I'm not going to lie—there were times when I had wished I didn't know her. Serena was trouble, and I knew it the minute I laid eyes on her. But I realize now that I needed her in my life. Serena's story helped me discover my own. Her experience jolted me out of my stupor and pushed me to take control of the languorous, hollow life that I had lived until then. For that I will always remain in her debt.

I finished my undergraduate degree in the spring of 2008 from the University of Massachusetts, Amherst, which wasn't exactly an amazing school, but it was decent. Lots of kids landed some pretty good jobs on graduation. Unfortunately for me, the economic meltdown hit and all of a sudden it seemed like the world was disintegrating—stock markets around the world were crashing, banking institutions were failing, people were being laid off by the thousands, and the US government was hastily trying to put together bail-out packages to help those most in need. Career Services at Amherst University told me point-blank that finding a job would be close to impossible given my unexceptional academic record. They asked me to very seriously consider my options back home in India. In my darkest dreams I had not imagined moving back to India, the country that I had left as a child, and where my parents still lived.

I spent hours on end at Career Services, browsing through thick binders and books, attending one counselling session after another and scouring the Internet for jobs. As time went by, and Career Services stopped answering my phone calls, it began to sink in that moving back to India was the only viable option I had. I was an Indian citizen, with a below average GPA in an inconsequential major, with a substandard resumé and to top it all I lacked the necessary social skills to impress interviewers. I was below average on every score. Period.

I did try, I'll give myself that. I tried hard to get a damn job, probably harder than I had ever tried for anything in my life, because I really did not want to move back to India. The thought of going back, after spending my entire adult life in the US, to a country that had become alien to me was terrifying.

My life at university was by no means fabulous. Most people would have found it boring, but I derived a certain degree of happiness and enjoyment from it. So, my boyfriend Param was geeky and not very good in bed, and he was just another desi investment banker, and my so-called friends said I could do much better, but I did like him quite a bit, and I didn't want to leave him. Not to sound melodramatic or anything, but I was maybe even a little heartbroken. I was sad at the thought of leaving behind my American college life because for me there was peace in this existence. Most people on campus would just let me be, and that's all that I really wanted—to be left alone. I had a couple of friends and they were all right—the kind that provided mild entertainment when it was needed, there were a few bars and restaurants that I frequented, the classes weren't so bad either, in fact I actually enjoyed some of them. I would be exaggerating if I said I was brimming with happiness at Amherst, but I can whole-heartedly say that I was content, and it is only now that I realize what a special and amazing feeling that is.

I unceremoniously graduated without a job and spent the summer shuttling between my elder sister's home in Providence, Rhode Island, and Param's shoebox apartment in Hell's Kitchen, Manhattan, because I didn't have the cash to pay rent. Neither my sister nor Param was particularly helpful in the job search. My sister the academic super nerd, a PhD student at Brown University, and her husband the distinguished doctor encouraged me to enter academia, the only thing they knew. Academia was also the only thing I knew I did not want to do. Param, my boyfriend, who led the dreary banker's life, coming home at 3 a.m., was barely holding on to his own job. I desperately looked for work to no avail. By August it came to a point where my bank balance was nearing zero, and when I had to borrow money from Param for a cup of coffee, it became blatantly clear to me that it was time to go back to India.

My sister tried to make me feel better by telling me that my parents missed me and that they were growing old and needed me, but it didn't help. My parents bought me a one-way ticket to New Delhi and that was the end of my life as I knew it.

After spending eighteen hours on an Air India flight, the cabin of which reeked of body odour thinly camouflaged with cheap perfume, I found myself in New Delhi, in a lizard-infested guest room with no friends, no boyfriend, my savings exhausted on an unemployed summer. All right, I'm exaggerating. Things weren't all that bad. The guest room had one resident lizard, my parents were moderately stingy and my father was a powerful government official, so life wasn't terrible by any standard. In a small way it was nice to wake up every morning to a hot breakfast and endless cups of chai, and not have to worry about food, laundry or bills.

I was almost twenty-two, which according to my parents was a suitable age to get married. I expected them to bombard me with biodatas of eligible bachelors from good homes, listing their age, height, weight and annual salary. But surprisingly they were strangely calm about the whole marriage thing. They didn't even push me to find a job, or to apply to grad school, or, for that matter, to do anything constructive with my life. Of course, there were the occasional 'what-are-you-planning-to-do-with-your-life' conversations, when I was summoned by my father early in the morning, but the one thing I had done in college was to master the art of bullshitting, so these discussions weren't much of an ordeal.

I enjoyed spending time at home. We had a beautiful garden, a cute dog, and a cook whose food was tolerable. Patience had always been one of my virtues—I think it stemmed from lethargy—so I could deal with the slow pace of life in Delhi and the even slower Internet connection.

I had a few friends in town, from my convent school years, whom I located on Facebook, but most of them were enjoying the trappings of matrimony which to me at this age was a ludicrous thought.

My life was now pretty lame and I didn't particularly mind because I figured this city had nothing more interesting to offer, so I continued to wallow in my apathy till a job, boy or US visa pulled me out of it.

All in all, I think I was okay, most of the time my parents just left me to my own devices. Which was how I liked it. I wasn't happy—how could one be in this shithole?—but I wasn't sad either. The days passed me by, taking on a rhythm of sorts though I sometimes experienced a strange, inexplicable kind of despondency, a sense of nervous calm that often left me feeling lost. Now when I look back at that time, I realize that this was probably the lull before the crazy storm that was going to hit my life. I would have inadvertently continued on that pathetic path for a long while if I hadn't met Serena.

We met in the locker room of Soul, a trendy new health club and spa. My father, as a senior income tax officer, had been given complimentary membership in the hope that when collection time came around, Soul would be spared. My father being frugal made it a point to go daily, and since my mother had been complaining of my sedentary lifestyle and weight, I started accompanying him.

Soul was my first initiation into Delhi society, and I was quick to realize that it was more a hangout than a gym. Though everything was in place for a world-class gym—the equipment was state of the art, the trainers very professional—everyone always seemed to be chilling and hanging out, the small talk between sets and the laughter between reps lasted longer than the sets and reps themselves. The clientele of Soul consisted mainly of middle-aged men who arrived at the gym determined to work out, heading straight for the treadmills where they immediately broke into a fast run, arms flailing, heavy tummies heaving. The uncles, as I liked to call them, would lose steam soon after and then proceed to take rounds of the gym, shaking hands, slapping backs, exchanging stock tips and business gossip with all the other uncles. The aunties, the middle-aged women of the gym, were always dressed in their best. Designer work-out gear and diamonds were de rigueur. They wore the latest Serena Willams collection, paired with carefully chosen tennis bracelets, earrings and pendants, the jewels small enough to not get in the way, but big enough to be noticed.

The aunties spent far more time in the plush locker room. They preferred the steam baths and saunas, which gave them a temporary rosy glow of health, to the gym, where lifting weights was tedious and the general understanding was that the residue from the sweat could not possibly be good for the skin.

It was a known fact around town that the latest and juiciest gossip was exchanged at the ladies' locker room in Soul. This, coupled with the fact that a few young politicians and senior bureaucrats were regular members (courtesy the complimentary memberships), provided priceless networking opportunities. There was a sudden surge of applications for membership, making the membership process at Soul selective, which then led to even more applications. The social climbers, as they were referred to in the sanctuary of the ladies' locker room, had made it a matter of pride to gain membership. Soul was like the hottest nightclub in town with a very tough door.

I spent a significant amount of time in the locker room myself, waiting for my father to finish his hour-long brisk walk on the treadmill, as I detested working out, and it was better to while away time here than anywhere else. In the ladies' locker room I gathered bits and pieces of information and began to understand the social dynamics at play. There was the usual gossip about cheating spouses and businessmen who pretended to be living it up while their companies were being run to the ground. But every once in a while a scandal would rock the glitterati at Soul. Like when the son of a famous politician died—for weeks the women in the locker room could not make up their minds whether it was an accident, murder or, horror of horrors, suicide! Or when the daughter of one of the regular members was charged with driving her brand-new Audi out of the showroom and into the thick of a hit-and-run case. I didn't contribute to these heated discussions but always paid close attention so I could go home and share the gory details with my mother. I had never imagined the Delhi of my childhood had changed so much.

On one such day I was sitting in front of a mirror in one of the plush terry bathrobes that they gave members, slowly and liberally applying the fragrant body lotion that was also complimentary, when she came and stood next to me, presumably in search of the highly popular lotion. I looked up at her and quickly looked away because she was completely naked except for a bright red panty adorned with a black bow.

Her overt friendliness was bordering on scary. 'Are you new here?' she asked me. Her words had a tinge of an American accent.

'Yeah, I am actually,' I replied, naturally looking up at her as I spoke, but then I had to avert my glance again given her nakedness, which she obviously had no qualms about.

'Oh, cool,' she said as she rubbed the lotion vigorously on her legs. 'New to Delhi as well? I haven't seen you around.'

'Um, yeah. I just moved here from the States.'

'Oh yeah?' I could sense the sudden interest. She blatantly looked me up and down, assessing me. Basic social etiquette prevented me from doing the same, but I observed her in the mirror out of the corner of my eye.

She was dark and her dull grey pallor was in stark contrast to her peroxide blonde hair which hung around her face in perfect, soft golden curls. She was chubby, with round buttocks and generous love handles that formed a soft roll around her tight red panty. She had nice large breasts, taut and firm. In a way the chubbiness suited her, making her look voluptuous rather than fat. She wasn't really attractive, but she wasn't hideous either.

She extended her hand, 'Hi, I'm Serena, nice to meet you.' I limply shook her hand and smiled at her weakly, 'Hi, I'm Riya.' She smiled back, a nice, friendly smile that made her dull face glow.' So how do you like it here in Delhi? You know I was in the States as well. New York. Manhattan, you know. I lived there for five years. I went to NYU, you know NYU, right? I'm sure you know New York University, everyone knows it. But don't worry, moving back is a shock at first and the adjustment will take time, but, you know, there are lots of good people here in Delhi . . . and lots of cute guys,' she said, winking at me.

She had a loud voice and spoke with a strange accent—a mix of a Punjabi and an American accent. She seemed like the kind of person who would say 'anyways'. 'You likin' it here? Have you made friends?' she asked, actually pausing for me to answer before continuing to rub the lotion into her arms.

'Kind of, I guess,' I replied tentatively. There was a moment of awkward silence and then I added, 'To be honest, I don't know many people here.'

She laughed. It was a hearty, loud, brassy laugh, a man's laugh. I didn't think I had said anything particularly funny, but it was nice hearing her laugh, it broke the awkwardness of the situation.

'Oh, nice, that's just like me . . . I lived there for five years, you know, in New York City . . . and wow did I love that city! I truly miss it, from the bottom of my heart! What a rocking city it is, na?' Now that she had finished applying lotion, the bottle half empty and her body glistening, she lit a cigarette, all the while looking at me, sizing me up. I could feel it, and I wriggled uncomfortably under her gaze. She took a long drag of her cigarette, blowing out a thin stream of smoke through her mouth and nostrils. It looked tempting, that cigarette of hers, it had been a while since I had smoked.

She said to me in a serious tone that made me look up at her, 'Well, sweetie, I was new here too, and now I'm not new any more. Don't worry, babe, it's a tough city, but you have me now, and I know that we are going to be very good friends.'

As simply as that Serena Sharma became my first friend in Delhi and a fixture in my life. The loneliness of the city drew us together, an unlikely pair.

Serena and I got along well, she liked to talk, and I liked to listen. Truth be told, I didn't have very much to say. So far I had led a fairly uneventful life and couldn't recall any stories that might interest her. I was happy to be regaled and shocked by Serena's colourful experiences. She enjoyed talking, and could go on for hours if she had an audience.

I found myself hanging out a lot with Serena because time passed by quickly when I was with her. She was always entertaining and, also, I didn't really have any other friends. Our nights came to take on a routine. I would have dinner with my parents, and by the time they'd retired for the night, Serena would come pick me up in her old rickety as she liked to call the dilapidated car she drove. We would go to one of the twenty-four-hour coffee shops and drink beer and smoke cigarettes. Sometimes when she had a joint, we would smoke the hash in her car and then go eat. Those were the best nights. Serena would order rajma chawal, and I would get chocolate chip pancakes. Serena would start off on one of her stories in her brash voice, and I'd spend the rest of the night giggling.

Serena loved to party. I came to realize that her life revolved around parties. I am not exaggerating if I say that the larger part of Serena's time was spent preparing for, and in anticipation of, the parties she would attend every weekend. She would strategically spend time at the right restaurants and health clubs and mingle with the right crowd, and inevitably some guy would invite her to a party. She always took me along because she couldn't go alone. I was only happy to have somewhere to go to.

Serena was truly addicted to the Delhi social scene. She would devour the page 3 columns in the newspapers with her morning breakfast. She prided herself on knowing the juiciest Delhi gossip and was a regular contributor to the stories at Soul. She would tell me about the glitziest weddings of the season, who had bought a private jet recently, who was wearing fake diamonds and who was carrying an imitation Louis Vuitton handbag. Even though I didn't personally know any of the people Serena spoke about, I derived cheap thrills from hearing about the tales of the rich and famous because they truly amazed me. I had never imagined that I of all people could be remotely close to anything in the slightest bit glamorous.

With Serena, I found myself seeing and experiencing Delhi in ways I hadn't believed possible. In all my years away I had thought of Delhi as I had left it, dusty and lethargic, where everything seemed to move in slow motion even to a child. In the Delhi of my childhood, entertainment was hanging out at the old-world Gymkhana Club that always smelt of pesticides, chaat parties in dusty lawns, which inevitably gave me chronic tonsillitis, and the occasional treat of dining at a restaurant in a five-star hotel—the life my parents, well-respected members of the civilized bureaucratic society, still led.

Much had changed since I had moved away. There were new roads, skyscrapers and steel-and-glass malls everywhere. But they all seemed transient, like they would soon lose their shine and fall apart. Plastic hoardings advertised affordable health insurance, the smiling faces of politicians, familiar signs of Western fast food. For how long would it all remain polished? India's heat, dust and rain would wear away all the gloss, leaving everything rusted, corroded and full of gaping holes.

The people here seemed to love plastic. The poor carried their possessions in colourful, meticulously preserved plastic bags. For the rich, plastic designer sunglasses provided protection from the grime and poverty pervading their wealthy neighbourhoods. Shielding their eyes from the flimsy plastic bags littering the gutters, the privileged remained in the sterile world they had created for themselves.

Slowly, I, too, became immune to the disfigured beggar, the naked child, the starving puppy. It was just easier that way.

Serena

That night we had gone to my friend Kamaya's place. We usually booked a hotel room or went to his guest house, but on that occasion we couldn't wait and Kamaya had offered her small apartment in Lajpat Nagar. The grimy bedroom was infested with lizards and ants, and reeked of cheap perfume. We drank the White Mischief vodka that Kamaya had in her freezer and snorted the cocaine that he kept in a small vial in his pocket. I cut the lines with his platinum credit card while he rolled a thousand-rupee note into a pipe. He only snorted through thousand-rupee notes. I remember the night fondly, despite the lizards and the dirty bathroom and the grimy sheets.

We didn't make love. Making love was what Salman and I did, where the sex itself was secondary, where every kiss, every caress, every action implied something profound—our bodies connecting on a deeper level. With Amar, it was different. I couldn't quite understand it, and I usually understood these things. I might not know much, but I am smart about things like sex. That is not to say it was just about sex with Amar, there was more to it. In a way I did love Amar, but it wasn't the kind of unwavering affection and passion that I had felt for Salman.

I will always remember the morning after. I woke up in Kamaya's bed, the sheets tangled around my naked body. It was still early, but Amar was dressed and ready to leave. Seeing I was awake, he brought his face close to mine as if to kiss me, but all he did was look deeply into my eyes, as if he was truly seeing me for the first time. He continued to stare at me, the expression on his face unfathomable. And then he kissed me on the cheek and said thank you, like he always did, before he walked out of the door.

After Amar left I wondered what he would tell his wife today. Maybe that's why he left early, so he wouldn't have to be interrogated when he got home. He became really nervous sometimes, especially after coke, and he would then start pacing back and forth. 'What do I tell her?' he would say to himself over and over again. He would grab his hair from the roots and pull hard. In the beginning, his behaviour used to scare me. I really thought I had done something wrong. I would try my best, even though I was frightened and nervous, to make him feel better. I would hug him and kiss him and hold him, but he would push me away.

I was smarter now. I understood him. I sometimes felt that there was no one in the world who understood him better than I did. Because I knew where he was coming from, I was able to forgive him. I realized that however hard he tried acting like a bad boy, he was soft inside. He was like an overgrown teenager who went through life acting on impulse, not realizing he was hurting people along the way. It was difficult to forgive a grown man like one forgives a child, but I could sense his restlessness and it helped me deal with him. I don't think his wife understood that about him. I could now deal with his anxiety attacks, just as long as I had a joint or a few drinks or even some Charlie to distract me.

I wanted to love Amar, I wanted to be there for him all the time, to help him with the loneliness and pain that I saw in his eyes. But how could I? I wasn't his wife, I wasn't even his girlfriend. What was I to him, I wondered sometimes.

It was the incredible sex and the excitement of an illicit affair that had initially drawn me to Amar. I had promised myself I wouldn't fall for this love bullshit again, not after what had happened with Salman. I was hurting and I needed a distraction. Amar was perfect—with him I didn't have to think, I could just let myself go and revel in the sensations of sex and cocaine. I knew I wasn't capable of falling in love like that again. But before I knew it, spending time with Amar had become more than just a source of pleasure. I reminded myself time and again that I had to stay strong and understand this for what it was—Amar was married, he had a wife and a newborn son, and he loved them. To him our relationship was only about sex . . . though he did tell me once that he loved me. At the time I believed him, but in moments of sanity doubts would surface. I would realize it could have been the alcohol and coke speaking that night.

I knew the only reason I was thinking this way was that I hadn't seen him for more than a week. I had to meet Amar tonight. He had left for London the day after we had met at Kamaya's and I missed him the entire time he was gone. But he was supposed to return today and I knew he'd be at F Bar. A week away from the Delhi social scene was more than he could handle. I knew I had to be there too.

The only problem was my friend Vik was throwing a party tonight and I had promised I'd go. Maybe I could talk him and his friends into going to the club after his party. But I knew that Vik didn't like nightclubs very much, he preferred hanging out with his coke-head friends and the random firang girls he was always surrounded by. I didn't like Vik all that much because I felt like I *had* to snort coke when I was with him. He never took no for an answer. Don't get me wrong, I enjoyed the sweet sugar, but there were times it made me anxious and my heart would beat really fast. I hated that feeling. The last time it had happened, Vik had smiled and told me it was normal. He then gave me a pill which he said would calm me down, make me less jittery. I don't remember how I got home afterwards. The pill knocked me out for over twenty-four hours. I had slept for so long that my mother, who usually never entered my room, had actually come in to ask if everything was okay.

But, I had promised Vik, and I have to admit his parties could sometimes be fun. And after that maybe Riya and I could go to F Bar and I'd get to meet my man.

I stared at my ghostly face in the mirror, all one uniform shade from the thick layer of foundation that I had applied. I reached for the blusher to add colour to my cheeks. Then the eyeshadow—I prefer darker shades, dark blues and greys, sometimes even black. I feel they make my eyes look smoky and glamorous. I used mascara to lengthen my short eyelashes, and then the most important part of my make-up routine—kajal, which I applied liberally. Soon it would spread giving my eyes a sexy, messy look. I rubbed scented oil on my body, and then reached for the short black dress that lay freshly ironed on the bed. The neckline of the dress revealed my generous cleavage and accentuated my breasts, making them look voluptuous. The short skirt displayed my legs to advantage. I slipped my pedicured feet into golden stilettos, grabbed my car keys and quietly slipped out.

My mother and stepfather were still awake, but I didn't say bye. I didn't like my stepfather seeing me all dolled up like this. Not like he was a perv or anything, but he was only fourteen years older than me. I mean I had dated guys his age. As I passed my parents' room, I heard him cooing lovingly to Tanya. He loved that baby so much—it made me sad when I saw them together, father and daughter. It reminded me of Papa.

I took the elevator—an old-fashioned one with a rusty iron grille door—which creaked dangerously as it made its way down to the ground floor. The young guard stared at me, looking me up and down, his gaze lingering on my legs. I shot him my dirtiest look, our eyes meeting for a brief second before he looked away with a hint of a smile on his lecherous face.

Outside, the air felt thick and heavy with moisture. The monsoon was my favourite season. There was something beautiful and sad about the grey clouds which would wreak havoc for short spells. I walked to my old rickety and tugged at the jammed door which opened with a creak. It was Papa's old car that I had inherited. It had caused a stir when he'd bought it—the Maruti Esteem was considered a luxury car back then. Everyone in Chandigarh had wondered how a police officer could afford such a car. He must be corrupt, they all said, but I knew the truth. Papa was an honest officer—he always had been—but he was a spendthrift, just like me.

I hit the accelerator to dispel these thoughts about Papa and the car let out a groan. I drove through the streets of Lutyens' Delhi to pick up Riya. In this part of the city everything looked the same. The wide streets were lined with huge green trees, the buildings were low and flat, their whitewashed walls sparkling in the moonlight. I could catch glimpses of the spacious bungalows behind the bamboo gates painted green and over the low red-brick walls. Street names were written in English, Hindi, Urdu and Punjabi on concrete arrow-shaped signboards. There was something wonderful about this part of Delhi. For the people who were in the know, it reeked of money, influence and class. Those who weren't could never even imagine the kind of wealth and power that existed here.

I reached Riya's house and gave her a missed call like she'd asked me to. While I waited for her in the car I redid my make-up. I then reached for the nearly empty perfume bottle that lay in the glovebox and spritzed myself. I took out a cigarette from the case, struck a match and lit it. As I sucked on the filter, I felt the smoke travelling down my throat and filling my lungs. I slowly let it out through my mouth. The first drag was always the best. I can clearly remember my first cigarette. The way the smoke had stung the back of my throat had been painful and it had brought tears to my eyes. Much had changed since then—I now smoked a pack a day. I laughed to myself, who could have ever imagined that my life would turn out this way.

Riya

It was a Friday, and as I had expected, Serena had plans for us. I was very bored when she called. I had spent most of the afternoon watching Hindi soap operas with my mom as I unenthusiastically searched online for jobs. Due to my sheer boredom and utter despondency, I found myself excited about the night that lay ahead.

Serena came to pick me up in old rickety. I had asked her to wait outside the gate while I sneaked out. Once in the car I offered to be the designated driver. Serena merely laughed and said, 'Honey, do you think you're still in America? These things don't matter here. We're all experts at drinking *and* driving. In fact, I drive better when I'm a bit drunk.' She then looked in the rear-view mirror, carefully rearranging a strand of blonde hair, and lit another cigarette.

She told me we were going to her friend Vik's house for a party, and afterwards we could possibly go to a nightclub. I shrugged, I was just happy to be out of the house.

We left central Delhi, and were soon driving down a road that was Delhi's version of a freeway. Serena drove fast—well, as fast as that beat-up old car would let her—weaving between big, noisy trucks, motorcycles and cars. She only slowed down when we entered what she called the farm area. This was where most of Delhi's fabulous parties were held, she assured me. It didn't exactly look like farmland, just a more uncivilized version of where we had come from. The potholed roads were flanked by empty tracts of land where stray cows and dogs roamed amidst plastic bags, waxy biscuit wrappers and shiny silver packets of paan masala. Serena turned on to a dusty lane and we were soon driving down a narrow dimly lit road with high walls on either side. In the gaps between the walls were small shanties lit by single light bulbs that sold bags of chips, packets of cigarettes, paan masala and cheap sweets. I was surprised to see one lean-to that had only eggs. Who the hell bought eggs at this hour? Serena just laughed, 'They're making anda-bread, you firang. Not everyone can afford a coffee shop.' She had started calling me firang—foreigner—as a term of endearment.

We soon approached a long long line of fancy cars. There were Mercs, Beamers and Audis everywhere. I think I even spotted a Porsche. To be honest, in America I wouldn't have given these cars a second glance. But here, on these dusty, beat-up roads, these machines were shiny symbols of wealth.

Serena had filled me in on Vik on the drive over. He was a very wealthy bachelor with two illegitimate children whom he loved. These were his kids from two different mothers. They were coke children, he joked, conceived during times when he and his partner were so stoned and overcome by passion that they had forgotten to use a condom. One of the children was half Nigerian, the other half German. They lived with their mothers in Goa and Vik saw to their every need. He tried being a good father; both children flew to Delhi every other weekend and stayed with their grandparents. Vik had tried having them over at his house, but his lifestyle wasn't very conducive to children. He was Delhi's unofficial drug lord and his house always had trays of cocaine, weed, ecstasy. Whatever drug you fancied, Vik would generously make it available. Spreading the love is what he called it.

Serena told me she wasn't very sure what Vik did to earn a living, if he did anything at all. He never seemed to work, though he often made trips to Nigeria. Rumour had it that Vik's father was one of Nigeria's biggest arms dealers. Ostensibly they manufactured cigarettes and alcohol and had factories and distilleries in Nigeria where labour was cheap. They sold everything under the brand 'Africana'. Their tagline, which was printed on the bottles and cartons, was 'Made for Africans, by Africans, in Africa'. Advertising was cheap and they had flooded the local channels. Soon Africana became very popular and they raked in the money. Serena told me she had once taken a sip of Africana whisky against Vik's advice. It was strong and disgusting, and tasted of petrochemicals.

We strategically parked old rickety away from the house so that no one would see us drive in or out. We walked unsteadily on the uneven gravel, passing cars with sleeping drivers and a line of bored valets looking clownlike in their ill-fitting white-and-red uniforms and funny hats. Serena wobbled precariously on her high heels and I walked a safe distance away from her in fear that she would tumble and take me down with her.

The house we walked towards was hidden from view by high walls. The imposing black gate was opened for us only after our names had been checked against the guest list by one of the four guards who stood at the gate, clad in a navy-and-gold uniform. The house was palatial, in fact I had never entered a house as grand as this before. We walked up the long cobbled driveway which was full of cars fancier than the ones we'd passed on our way to the gate: Bentley Arnages, Porsches and one Lambhorgini Countach. On either side of the driveway were expansive manicured lawns that were adorned with numerous stone sculptures and fountains, all dimly lit by floodlights. The lawns seemed endless and I couldn't tell where they stopped. I felt uncomfortable in the ill-fitting skirt and spaghetti that I was wearing. Perhaps I should have worn something more glamorous, but then this was the only outfit left in my wardrobe that I hadn't worn to one of these parties. I made a mental note to go shopping—if I planned to continue partying with Serena I'd need more clothes.

The house had wide marble steps that led up to the front door, the kind they have at hotel entrances. Serena's stilettos clacked against the hard surface shattering the silence of the night. It was only then that I realized I couldn't hear any party sounds—no music, no voices, no laughter. There was absolute silence save for the sounds of the night—the distant rumbling of a truck, the chirping of a cricket, the sputter of a passing scooter.

As we approached the heavy oak doors, they were flung open by a tall, lanky man with pale, pock-marked skin. His long, greasy hair was streaked with silver. I figured this was Vik.

He saw Serena and laughed, 'Welcome to the temple.' From behind him an accented voice added, 'Of sin,' which prompted drunken laughter that could be heard over the pulsing music. I wondered how thick the doors were not to have let any sound escape. Vik was holding a silver tray, the kind my mom used for her daily puja. On the tray were rose petals, and a white heap of cocaine.

Serena introduced me as 'Riya from America'. Vik kissed us both on either cheek in the European fashion. I had come to realize that this was the norm in Delhi.

Vik waved the tray under Serena's nose, trying to entice her. She just crumpled her nose in distaste and laughed. But this wasn't her usual confident, brassy laughter; it was high-pitched and tinged with nervous undertones. Vik rolled his eyes at her. 'As boring as ever, Ms Sharma.'

'Too early in the night, my friend,' Serena replied as we walked into the house.

There were about a hundred people inside and there were waiters serving cocaine, acid and E in trays like Vik's. We passed an opulent dining room where an elaborate dinner had been set out. The aromas made my stomach rumble, but I figured it would be a serious faux pas if I ate right away.

'Can I offer you a drink?' Vik asked me as we made our way to the bar, which like the rest of the house was also over the top. It ran down the length of the room and was armed with three bartenders who stood fully gloved and uniformed in black and white. It seemed that Vik had a thing for uniforms. 'Two vodkas with Red Bull for the ladies and a large Gold Label for me,' said Vik.

A tall, skinny girl came up to Vik and hugged him. She was surely a model, though she wasn't very pretty. Her legs went on forever and she had a short stylish haircut. There was something about the way these models carried themselves that set them apart from everyone else. Vik loved models and entertained them regularly. I wondered why he gave someone like Serena the time of day, especially when he seemed to be surrounded by beautiful women of every nationality. But then I guess Vik had a lot of time. I watched Serena take a sip of her drink, her red nail colour matching the red stain her mouth left on the glass. She was decent looking but nowhere in the same league as these other women. But as I kept looking I saw her expression change, a huge smile lit up her face, transforming it, making her beautiful. She squealed in delight. 'One sec, babe, I'll be right back. I just saw a very good friend and I must go say hello,' she said before running towards the door.

I was left alone, and I looked around at all the people. We were in a big room with French windows that led out to a massive swimming pool. I felt out of place, I didn't know anyone and most of the people were too drunk or high to carry on a conversation, not that I would ever have the courage to initiate one. So I kept sipping my drink. I, too, wanted to feel the buzz, so I drank quickly, taking long sips through the straw. The vodka stung, leaving behind a trail of heat down my throat that slowly seeped through my body.

Before I could even ask, the waiter brought me another drink. Vik and the giggly model were still standing next to me, though they seemed to have forgotten my presence. Serena had vanished into the crowd, and from where I stood I couldn't see her anywhere. The alcohol was hitting me fast now and I was getting really buzzed. I was having a great time drinking and just being by myself.

Usually when I drink a lot, I feel really sleepy, and I had soon reached this point. All that vodka had sedated me, and I found my eyes fluttering and my words slurring. Serena had returned at some point in the evening. I was trying to focus on her face to still my spinning head, but my attention was drawn to Vik. He was separating a heap of cocaine into lines with a credit card. He smiled at me and told me to give it a try. His smile dazzled me, his teeth were as white as the coke and I saw a gold tooth glistening. Funny, I hadn't noticed it before.

I tried telling him I didn't do cocaine, but he just laughed and said, 'I love introducing virgins to the pleasures that the Lord has bestowed upon us—the pleasures of nature and life.'

'Cocaine is hardly natural!' I retorted.

Vik laughed and threw a handful of the white powder in the air and I watched fascinated as it drifted down like sparkly snowflakes.

I took a five-hundred-rupee note that Serena had rolled into a pipe and followed her suit. I held my hair back, put the pipe to my nose and snorted, moving the pipe along the length of the white line, inhaling every little bit.

The coke burned my nostrils and suddenly I was wide awake, more alert than I had been all night, and I felt totally sober. It was like the cocaine had mitigated the drowsy effects of the alcohol, jolting me back to the real world. My brain had never felt this sharp ever before. Words rang out loud and clear, I could hear the clink of glasses, the music seemed louder and I could feel the bass pumping through my body. I was in complete control of myself, each sensation clearer and more fantastic. And then I did another line.

In the short time that Serena was part of my life we attended many parties. Most of them are a hazy blur, but this particular one stands out. At the time it was a night to be celebrated—my first time doing cocaine—but now it is a reminder of the path my life could so easily have taken.

Serena and I sat together by the pool in the dazed aftermath of the party, enjoying our last drink, a toast to the breaking dawn. Serena was recalling a similar wild party that she had been to in New York and I was only half listening when she suddenly fell quiet. I looked up to see what had caused her to stop her monologue. I still remember his eyes—hard and piercing, they were fixed on her. He wasn't very tall, but he held himself high. He was definitely handsome, better looking than any of the other men around. He was fair and his most striking feature was his sharp, aquiline nose. The man's black hair, a nice contrast to his fair skin, was gelled back. The thing is he looked like an asshole.

He was headed straight for us, and without even so much as sparing me a glance, he pulled Serena up by the arm and held her close. 'Amar!' she giggled. 'What are you doing?' But as he pulled her away, she followed willingly, almost tripping over herself to catch up with him. So this was the guy she was always talking about. I watched them disappear into the house before turning to examine my wavering reflection in the pool. I marvelled at how different I looked. It was as if I was a different person from the one who had walked through those grand oak doors a few hours ago. I had enjoyed myself tonight and couldn't wait for the next party. The coke had changed me—I'd never imagined I'd like it so much. I don't know how long I sat there contemplating this change before Serena returned.

'Oh my God, babe, isn't he hot? That's my man, my Amar,' she said.

'I guess, though he looked like an asshole to me,' I replied honestly.

She laughed loudly. 'He is a bloody asshole, but a really good-looking one.'

Serena

I woke up feeling like shit. It was 3 p.m. and I didn't want to get out of bed. I wished I could go back to sleep and never wake up. I closed my eyes, but sleep evaded me. I was very uncomfortable because I had gone to sleep in my underwear and the wire in my bra was poking me. My brain told me I needed food though my stomach was numb. I thought of all the things I loved to eat—rajma chawal, cheesy pizza, chocolate pudding—but that just made me nauseous. I finally got out of bed. My head started spinning. I sat on the edge of my bed with my head in my hands till it stopped. My mouth was dry, and I reached for a bottle of water and took a sip. The water made my stomach churn. I found my favourite blue cotton pyjamas, the ones with pink hearts on them, in a pile on the floor. I wanted to rinse the taste of cigarettes and vodka out of my mouth and wash the smell of smoke from my hair, but I couldn't stand up. My body hurt too much. What was the point of getting out of bed, anyways? I had no one to talk to. I hated the daytime. I rarely saw any of my friends during the day and I sometimes wondered if I would even recognize them if I did.

At times like these, when I felt like total shit and I missed Papa, I always thought of Salman. I thought of his cute button nose, the round, dorky photochromatic glasses that he wore, how he always smelt of cumin. God, I had loved him so much, I had loved him more than anyone else. I never completely understood why he stopped loving me.

All the sad, terrible memories came flooding back. I had confronted him the day I found him in bed with that woman. He told me that he had stopped loving me a long time ago. I was devastated. All my dreams of Salman and me starting a happy family had come crashing down. I returned home to find my parents divorced. It had been all too much to deal with at that time. And then Papa died. I knew I had changed since then. I no longer dreamt of learning to cook three-course Indian meals for my family. I didn't even want a family any more. I wasn't looking for a husband. The men I now sought out were the complete opposite of Salman—like Amar. He was smart, successful, rich and married. I told myself I liked the fact that Amar wasn't single. That way we couldn't be in a regular relationship and I'd never get my heart broken again.

Riya

Fuck. What had I done last night? My body felt shattered.

This was surprising because yesterday I had felt wonderful. I had done line after line of coke since I didn't feel it hitting me. All it did was wake me up. But now I felt like death. I couldn't move my body, my throat hurt, my gums felt raw. Worst of all, I couldn't feel my stomach—it was completely numb. I wanted to get out of bed and drink some water, my mouth was dry and my tongue stuck to the roof of my mouth, but I couldn't deal with it. I guess cocaine worked differently from alcohol. I just wanted to lie down with my arms wrapped around my stomach forever. I drifted in and out of sleep, letting my mind wander in a dreamlike state. I thought of Param, I realized I missed him intensely. I thought of Amherst—of the crisp, fall air slapping my face, the patches of warm sun that trickled through the trees, the Irish pub that smelt of beer and sawdust where my shoes always stuck to the floor, my small dorm room which I had decorated with colourful wall hangings from Janpath. I thought of last night. All those random people who were actually not that snooty, though I was so fucked I wouldn't have been able to tell the difference. I suddenly had a hazy recollection of a guy slobbering all over me. I think we had been talking for a few minutes when he started kissing me and running his hands all over my body. And I didn't try to stop him even once. I was horrified and disgusted with myself. How could I have made out with a complete stranger at a party?

At this point all I wanted to do was to go back to sleep and wake up to being the old Riya, the one who was quiet and kept to herself. My mother knocked at my door, asking if I was okay. I told her I had my period so she wouldn't bother me any more. Anyway my voice sounded strained because of the physical discomfort I was feeling. Of course I had been drunk before, I had often nursed a hangover in college. But this was a whole new level of suffering. I was falling into a restless sleep again when I felt my cellphone vibrate next to me. Probably Serena calling to tell me how fucked she felt.

Serena

Karan was coming into town today. It was perfect timing because my parents were in Chandigarh for the weekend. I thought of Karan and I smiled, fond memories flooded my mind. I have known him since I was five years old, Papa and Karan's father were inducted into the civil service in the same year. On my annual trips back home, when Papa was posted in London and later when I was in New York, I would always meet Karan in boring old Chandigarh. Back then he was a round, chubby, unattractive boy with a turban that was too big for his small head. Then Karan hit puberty, he lost weight, cut his waist-length hair, and his shrill voice became deep and sexy. I always thought he was nice and we would flirt when I was in town during my summer break. We would speak on the phone late into the night and I would tell him about New York and Salman and I could sense the jealousy in his voice. I thought Karan was young and silly and sweet. I even recalled my sexual experiences with Salman and he had listened curiously. Later he told me that hearing my voice on the phone he longed for me, imagining me naked.

Things changed overnight when I came back from New York. I was single and heartbroken and soon after my return Papa died. I needed someone . . . I desperately wanted someone to help me forget the pain. Karan was there, faithful and loyal as ever, and I had turned to him for solace. We lived together for nine months in Papa's house while Ma and Randeep were in Delhi. I had taught Karan everything I knew about making love. With every touch, every caress, he learnt how to be a better lover.

I hadn't met him since I moved to Delhi and now he was here. I wore sexy lacy underwear and a short red dress that complimented my blonde hair. I parked my car outside his hotel and waited for him. He looked so handsome as he walked towards me, the stubble dark against his fair skin, his eyes twinkling below his thick eyebrows. He was dressed in baggy jeans and a loose shirt, the open buttons revealing his chest. He got into the car and gave me a big kiss.

'Serena, you look fabulous,' he said, his hand on my thigh.

'Thanks, babe, you don't look so bad yourself,' I replied playfully and winked at him. He ran his smooth hand down my bare legs. I laughed and slapped his hand away.

We made small talk as we drove back to my place. I asked him about common friends back in Chandigarh. I even asked about his family, his parents whom I had known my entire life had always treated me like their own . . . until I started dating Karan. They didn't approve of our relationship, he was their only son, and I was an orphan—the daughter of a fallen mother and a dead father.

I hadn't gone back to Chandigarh, there were too many unpleasant memories there—my parents' bitter divorce, Papa's death. I moved to Delhi and started a new life. I wanted fresh beginnings, my past had died with Papa.

We reached my house and the minute my room door closed behind us, Karan grabbed me by the waist. He was strong now and had been working out. 'Hello, gorgeous,' he had said in that way of his, and looked at me with his playful eyes twinkling. I grabbed his shoulders, wider than I remembered, as he kissed me. It was just like before. The kiss felt comfortable, comforting. I knew the shape of his mouth, the texture of his tongue. I knew exactly when he would start rolling his tongue around my mouth, when he would reach for my bra. It was like clockwork.

Sad memories flooded my mind as we made love. I had lived in Chandigarh after Papa's death desperately holding on to Karan, fearing what would happen if I let go. Even though I didn't love Karan, I had lived for him because I had nothing else to live for.

The buzzing of the phone woke me up in the middle of the night—it was Amar. He was fucked, I could hear it in his voice. He asked me to meet him, and I almost said yes, but then I noticed Karan standing quietly by the window, drinking a beer.

'Amar, darling, not tonight, I'm busy.' As I said his name I saw Karan stiffen. Amar hung up without saying goodbye. He could be such a child sometimes. He was angry and I didn't know what to do. But I knew Amar, and I knew that like a child, he just needed time, he would call me soon enough. For the moment there was Karan.

Karan left early the next morning, tiptoeing his way through my parents' apartment. Ramu was in the kitchen making a cup of tea, and he smirked when he saw Karan leaving. I hated his guts, but I tipped him generously so that he wouldn't tell Ma. After Karan left, I went back to my room, closed the door and smoked a cigarette. I never smoke when I am with Karan, he doesn't like the taste of cigarettes. I had asked him to do Charlie with me, I had told him that it was the best feeling ever, but Karan didn't do drugs. He had given me a sad look when I had snorted. Instead of using crisp thousand-rupee notes, which I didn't have, I had placed a small heap of coke on a credit card and snorted the entire thing. It hit me right away. To be honest, I didn't really want to do it, but I wanted to prove something to Karan, to show him how cool I was.

I don't know why I felt this need to project myself as cosmopolitan. It was like the time I had cheated on Salman. And it happened only because I had suspected him of sleeping with someone else.

Salman and I had a fight and I was at a nightclub, getting drunk. Salman hated clubs, though I really enjoyed them. I was having a fun time dancing with my friends that night when I met Abdullah.

He had the biggest table at the club and was popping bottle after bottle of champagne. He wasn't cute, but there was something about him that I found attractive, maybe it was because he looked wealthy. I noticed him looking at me more than once and finally, after a couple of drinks, I went up to him and said hello. His English was heavily accented, I barely understood what he said, especially over the loud music, but I nodded and smiled at him anyways. He offered me a glass of champagne and I accepted with a smile. I loved champagne and didn't get a chance to drink it often enough. Salman wasn't much of a drinker and usually stuck to beer.

Abdullah and I danced a lot that night. He kept refilling my glass and he held me by the waist as we danced. He smiled at me a lot, and I decided that I liked him. At the end of the night I went with Abdullah and his friends to his hotel room. I rode in the front seat of Abdullah's small red sports car. I had never driven in a car like this before and

I felt like royalty. Who knew, maybe Abdullah *was* royalty. He had the best table in one of New York's poshest nightclubs and was surrounded by wealthy, beautiful people.

I was really drunk by the time we got to his hotel. I could barely see straight as I gazed at the mirror. I was wearing a sexy dress that night, one that Salman had gifted me. I was also wearing my fake diamond earrings and when I looked into the mirror, I saw the image of a girl who I imagined frequented the best nightclubs, bought expensive clothes and wore exquisite jewellery . . . tonight that girl was me. I was impressed with Abdullah's luxurious suite in the trendy Meatpacking district. Waiters served expensive wine and champagne to beautiful women dressed in designer clothes. If I had stayed at home that night Salman and I would have done the usual, boring couple things. I would have cooked his favourite Indian meal— butter chicken and biryani. We would have watched a Hindi movie, and if Salman didn't fall asleep, we would have made love. On nights when he felt energetic, we'd venture out to the twenty-four-hour Dunkin Donuts where I would drink a vanilla chai latte and together we'd dig into a box of Munchkins.

The owner of the store, a family friend of Salman's, would always tease us about marriage, and I'd blush and squeeze Salman's hand tightly.

As I looked around Abdullah's suite, I thought about how this was the life that I had always dreamt of. Beautiful people, amazing parties, lots of champagne.

Abdullah didn't speak much English, but he treated me well. He held me by the waist, made sure my glass was always full and kept smiling at me. After a while I got bored, everyone around me was talking in a foreign language, so I wandered off and stood on the balcony. I don't remember for how long I was out there, but when I returned to the room, everybody had left. I felt strange and uncomfortable and wanted to go back home. I was even missing Salman.

As I made my way to the door, Abdullah came up from behind and began kissing my neck. I tried stopping him, but I was very drunk and he was insistent. He turned me around to face him and kept kissing me as he took my clothes off. I was too tired to protest. Before I knew it we were on the bed and Abdullah was clumsily trying to force himself into me. He yelped and it was over. The whole episode had not lasted more than ten minutes and I hadn't felt a thing the entire time. We both passed out immediately afterwards.

I woke up early the next morning. In the daylight streaming into the room Abdullah looked ugly, he had a huge paunch and under his stubble his face was covered with acne. His naked body was sprawled across the bed and he was snoring loudly with his mouth open. I looked at his body in disgust, there were tufts of curly black hair everywhere. I quickly dressed and put on a sweater that I found lying on a chair. I could tell from the soft material brushing against my skin that it was expensive. I quietly left the room.

I cried on the subway ride home. What had I done? I had cheated on Salman, the man I loved, the man I was going to marry, the man whose children I would one day bear. I sobbed while everyone around me stared, but I couldn't stop. The first thing I did when I got home was take a morning-after pill. I always kept a couple, just in case Salman and I forgot to use a condom, though we never did forget, he was extra careful. I then took a shower. I had never felt so dirty. I washed the smell of smoke, alcohol and him off my skin.

I scrubbed away the memory of last night. Salman would never find out, he couldn't.

After my bath I called Salman and apologized for fighting. I asked him to come over and promised to make the butter chicken that he loved. He came immediately and we kissed and made love. He felt wonderfully warm inside me. Afterwards he asked me not to cook and took me out for lunch to our favourite Indian restaurant instead.

As we ate from the yellowed plates on a tablecloth stained with spots of pink and orange, laughing, talking and kissing, scandalizing the old aunties and uncles around us, the previous night seemed like a blurry, distant memory. It was as if it had happened to someone else.

Riya

Tonight was the celebrated fashion designer Dhruv Behl's pool party. It was the last pool party of the season, so it would definitely be rocking. Everyone who was a part of Delhi's page 3 circuit was going to be there.

Serena looked spunky tonight. She had her hair and make-up done at the parlour, her fluffy blonde hair fell in locks around her bronzed face, and her eyes were done in vivid shades of blue and black. She wore a tiny pair of dark blue denim shorts that ended right below her butt. They matched the blue of her eyeshadow. With the shorts she wore a white wife beater that revealed just a peek of her lacy blue bra. To complete the outfit she wore her highest pair of heels.

Tonight we were joined by Pinky. Serena had told me about her. She was thirty-six and very well connected. She knew everyone around town and Serena gleefully told me that being seen with her was the key to acceptance into this crowd. Pinky was the one who had introduced Serena to Delhi's inner circle and she would now do the same for me.

I was told the only way to be a part of this group was if you had money, power and fame. It was necessary to show off your wealth by throwing lavish parties, wearing designer clothes and building beautiful homes. It was important to play the name game at these parties, letting everyone know who you were and where you stood in the social hierarchy. Single women were the only exception. It just wasn't that difficult for girls in India. It wasn't like New York or Miami where there were hordes of hot single women. Here any unattached woman, whether she was good looking or not, was accepted. So it wasn't that tough for girls like Serena and Pinky because while the women ignored them, their husbands welcomed them.

We picked Pinky up on the way to the party and she and Serena complimented each other on their outfits. Pinky wasn't as provocatively dressed as Serena—she was wearing a short skirt and a black bikini bra over which she wore a white crochet top. As soon as we were on our way Pinky took out a small vial from her purse and sniffed. Her eyes watered and her nose turned red. She then took eyeliner and touched up the kajal that had smeared. Serena suggested that she use some foundation to hide the redness around her nose. Serena asked Pinky about her seven-year-old son. Pinky said he had gone to America with his father, and that he would be back in two days. She missed him and couldn't wait till he was back. She sighed and added that this was the end of her partying days, once her son arrived she would give it all up.

Serena had told me that Pinky often vowed to give up this lifestyle, she wouldn't go out for a week, but then she would itch for cocaine, alcohol and sex. She had lost faith in the institution of marriage shortly after hers fell apart a year after she and Gaurav had walked around the holy fire. They had been wildly in love. He was the man she was looking for, handsome, rich and fun. He owned nightclubs in Delhi, and she loved to party. She would laugh and tell her friends that she would party till she was fifty, by then all the cigarettes would kill her anyway. Gaurav was perfect—until they got married. That's when she began seeing the flaws, he was fat and dark, and severely in debt. To add to it, Delhi's new police commissioner made sure that nightclubs shut at midnight. Whatever money Gaurav had in the bank was squandered away by Pinky who took the baby and went to Europe to escape her worries. Gaurav had to sell his clubs to repay his debt and he now ran a small, shady bar in the suburbs of Delhi. He was soon forgotten by the people he once considered his friends. Pinky divorced him—she couldn't bear to be the wife of a social pariah. She got custody of her son and moved into her father's home. After the pain and anguish of the divorce Pinky vowed never to marry again. She then began associating with the high and mighty of Delhi—the men, that is.

We arrived at our destination—a sprawling farmhouse set amidst expansive green lawns, with two swimming pools around which groups of people stood drinking and chatting. As at all parties the men discussed business, trading tips, IPOs, property prices, while the woman talked about handbags, jewellery, holidays in St Tropez, the best clubs in London and the fanciest restaurants in Florence. The night was young, the music and the mood mellow.

Everyone knew this wouldn't last, the alcohol would fuel the crowd and the music would be drowned out by laughter. The young DJ knew exactly when to turn up the volume, he knew when the crowd would want hip-hop and techno to be replaced by brash Bollywood music. Bikinis and diamonds were in vogue this summer. The women, high heels sinking into the moist lawn, made their rounds of the crowd, smiling, kissing, sipping champagne.

Pinky and Serena knew several people at the party, and immediately began socializing. Serena left me, giving me a quick hug before she wandered off, 'Darling, you don't mind, do you?' Of course I didn't mind. I never did.

Serena

Pinky was talking to some lecherous old guy and I was getting bored. I decided it was time I said hello to the host of the party. I spotted Dhruv in the distance surrounded by a crowd of young men. Dhruv Behl was gay and very flamboyant. He always attended parties with a handsome young man on each arm. Tonight was his night, his moment in the spotlight, and there were many pretty young things milling around him. The boys loved the cool older man, and women loved the cute gay boys so they too would linger around Dhruv. He stood in the centre of the group, resplendent in his customary all-white garb, his cowboy hat and nubuck boots. His long silver hair was tied back in a ponytail to give a messy look.

I wasn't in the mood to brave the crowd hanging around Dhruv, so I stood at a safe distance while trying to locate someone to speak with. Suddenly I felt something creep up the back of my thigh. I jumped while trying to turn around at the same time. But my beautiful silver heels were stuck in the moist lawn and before I knew it, I had lost balance and was crashing to the ground. I closed my eyes, held my breath, fearing the inevitable . . . I was going to be the laughing stock of this party, caked in mud and grass. But just as I was about to hit the ground, close enough to smell the mud, I was rescued by a pair of strong arms. It was just like in the movies . . . I opened my eyes, my hair was blocking my vision. A gentle hand brushed a lock away and I found myself looking up at Amar's smiling face. I blushed, my heart skipped a beat like it always did when I saw him. I felt warm and cold and I felt my body tremble. He laughed as he helped me stand up. I pretended to be angry, I frowned and gently slapped him on the cheek. That just made him laugh louder.

'I want to tear your clothes off,' he said slowly. 'You look so edible tonight.' I smiled, Amar was so handsome. He got his fair complexion from his English mother and his dark hair from his Indian father. 'Darling,' he whispered in that fabulously husky voice of his, 'I've booked a room tonight at the Shangri-La. I'll see you there at around two.' He kissed me ever so lightly on the forehead, gently touched my neck, before walking away.

That evening I mingled as I always did. It was a crowd I knew well—it was always the same people at every party. The drinks were great, the little girls' room had plenty of Charlie and E. I had every reason to enjoy myself but I was unable to have a great time no matter how many glasses of champagne I drank. I was anxiously waiting for the night that lay ahead.

I lay in bed sweating because of the humidity, my air conditioner had conked off for the umpteenth time. I stared at the ceiling and the walls of my room—they were badly in need of a paint job. I thought of my house in Chandigarh, we had had one of the biggest government houses and Papa had hired an interior designer to decorate my room. It was a surprise when I returned from New York. There was a lovely four-poster bed, a quaint teak dressing table, a beautiful rug that my father had ordered from Agra. I didn't stay in that room for very long because soon after I returned Papa had the heart attack.

I had led the life of a princess in Chandigarh. I was the apple of my father's eye. I always got my way with Papa. I remember the extravagant birthday parties that he threw for me when I was a kid—there were clowns, elephants and everyone from my school was invited. When I was older he sat up with me as I pulled all-nighters studying for my exams. I remember how he cried when I boarded the plane to New York. God, I missed Papa. In a way I was glad he wasn't alive to see the outcome of my terrible break-up with Salman, to see my mother, the woman he had loved so dearly, married to another man, to see my mother give birth to another man's baby.

I desperately wanted a cigarette now. The sounds of laughter and people chatting floated into my room from outside. Randeep's sister was visiting with her family and I was not included in the fun. My mother had looked disappointed when I went outside to say hello to everyone. She was embarrassed, her sister-in-law was probably wondering how a beautiful woman like Parmeet had given birth to a daughter like me. There was an awkward silence when I had politely greeted them. I was a reminder of my mother's tainted past. I reminded Randeep's family of the fact that he had married an older woman, when as an intelligent, handsome civil servant he could have had his pick of beautiful young women. Not only was my mother ten years older than him, she also had a grown-up daughter whom he had to support.

I had taken off the uncomfortable salwaar kameez as soon as I had returned to my room. I felt so alone right now. It was strange to see my mother with her new family. Ma still loved me, I believed that, but it was different now. She wasn't the mother I remembered from my childhood, the one who loved our family more than anything else. She now had a new family—a new husband, a new child, a new home.

I hated it, especially on days like today, when it was evident that I wasn't a part of my mother's new family. I yearned for my father on such days. I had lived alone with Papa when I returned from New York. I had come home, devastated after my broken engagement, only to find that my parents were divorced. Ma had moved into her parents' house in Ludhiana and Papa was all alone. I liked living with him, taking care of him. It was very peaceful till Mrs Bhatia entered our lives. Even now, just the thought of that woman made me livid.

Mrs Bhatia was a widow whose husband had been killed in action in Kashmir soon after I had returned from New York. Colonel Bhatia was one of Papa's closest friends and after his death my father made sure his wife and children were comfortable.

But Mrs Bhatia was a conniving, disgusting woman. She slowly made herself a part of our lives. She came over every day and stayed till late at night drinking whisky with Papa in the study. I remember that dirty drunk, I remember how she had passed out on our sofa one night. I had found her sprawled there the next morning snoring, her long black hair a mess, her mouth wide open. I had run out of the house and wept. I didn't know what to do, I didn't know whom to turn to. I felt so wretched, my own father, the man whom I loved most in the world had turned against me, against our family. I wanted to call Ma, but I didn't want her to think badly of Papa. At that time I still harboured hopes that they would reunite. I knew I had to deal with the pain myself. There was only one person who would've understood me—Salman. But he didn't care any more, he didn't love me. Mrs Bhatia was a slut. I had heard her and Papa having sex in my parents' bedroom, on their bed. I had been woken up late one night by the creaking in the next room. I had blocked my ears with my fingers and buried my head in my pillow but it made no difference—I could still hear them.

After Papa died, I never saw Mrs Bhatia again. She didn't come to the funeral, she didn't even bother sending flowers.

Outside I heard everyone get up and leave for dinner. Ma hadn't invited me. I heard the front door close. I jumped out of bed, grabbed a cigarette and walked out to the balcony. I lit the cigarette and took a long, deep drag. Finally, peace.

Parmeet

A deathly silence loomed over the house. We sat quietly at the dining table eating slices of bread slathered with strawberry jam. There was no dinner tonight, in the midst of the chaos, I had forgotten to give Ramu instructions.

Half an hour ago Serena had stormed out of the apartment screaming and weeping. Randeep and she had fought again and this time it went completely out of control. She had complained about how she was neglected, how she never had enough money, how her car had broken down twice this week, how no one really cared about her. Randeep had been in a foul mood since he returned from office. Usually he was able to deal with Serena's bickering calmly, she was my daughter after all. Tonight, though, he had fought back, and the screaming had become louder, the arguments more bitter. Serena had turned to me for support, but this was a precarious situation for me and I chose not to get involved. I had calmly told her that they would have to sort it out themselves. It all ended when Randeep slapped her hard enough to turn her face red. He told her to get out of his house. He even screamed at me, and told me I would have to choose between Serena and him. He told me he didn't want Tanya growing up under her influence. The baby's howls didn't help the situation very much. I had never seen him this angry, he was a doctor and patience was his greatest virtue.

Before she stormed out, Serena also screamed at me. She told me this was *my* fault, I had ruined her life. 'Why did you marry him? Why did you have another child? Wasn't I enough?' She cried and demanded her share of SP's property.

I didn't lose my temper with Serena often, but this time she had crossed the limit. If Randeep hadn't slapped her, I would have done so myself. I told her to get the hell out of my house, because there wasn't any room in it for a girl like her.

How could I have produced such an ungrateful child? Serena had been trouble since the day she was born. She was a ten-pound baby, and the labour pains were terrible, far worse than with Tanya. She was so big and heavy and she had entered the world with a loud cry.

After Serena left the house, the mood was sombre. Tanya stopped crying and Randeep didn't say a word to me. I looked at him across the table as he read the newspaper and chewed on a slice of toast, the crumbs sticking to his prickly moustache.

He was so young, only thirty-seven, ten years my junior, but I loved him. For the first time in my life I had experienced what love actually was. I knew all along that he would stay with me, though everybody else had their doubts. Soon after he joined the Indian Administrative Service, we got married and on that day Tanya was conceived—a child born into a marriage of love, not one of convenience and coercion. Randeep was a strong, good man, if only Serena would realize that. He has done so much for her, he has done so much for all of us.

Randeep rose, brushed his face with the back of his hand and went into the bedroom. I stayed at the table, I knew he needed to be by himself for a while. I had wanted to throw Serena out, I really did, but the guilt didn't let me. After all those years of trauma, I had finally built a life for myself, a life I enjoyed. After all those years I felt the desire to wake up in the morning. Didn't every woman deserve that? For the first time in years I was happy, and now Serena was trying to sabotage my marriage and my new family. But every day the guilt ate at me. Had I ruined my daughter's life? Had it all been my fault? But after all the sadness I had felt while married to SP, didn't I deserve happiness as well? I had given birth to Serena when I was very young. I had raised her all these years. Wasn't that enough? How much longer would I have to bear the burden of this child?

Serena

I cried as I floated in the shallow end of the swimming pool. In this big pool my tears were just tiny droplets that didn't mean a thing. I was glad it was nearly empty and I steered clear of the few remaining swimmers as I swam underwater, the water stinging my eyes. I cried till there were no more tears.

How dare he slap me? He wasn't my father, he had no right to touch me. How dare he tell me to get out of the house? My mother didn't support me, she never did. She thought I was trying to sabotage their marriage, but that wasn't true, it wasn't true at all. I was happy for my mother, I was happy that the divorce came through and that she had found Randeep, he was a good man, I knew that.

As the water cleared my head I realized I had behaved awfully tonight. How could I be so cheap?

How could I ask my mother for property? How could I stoop so low? I loved Ma so much, she had given birth to me, raised me, taught me everything I knew. How could I treat her like this? I cried and cried, if only my Papa was still alive, none of this would have happened. Why had God done this to me? Why had He taken away everything that I loved? Oh, Papa, why did you have to go away leaving me with nothing?

There was a time when there were so many people who loved me and cared about me, and now my whole life lay shattered in front of me. After all the destruction it was difficult for me to hold on to the scary roller-coaster that my life had become and often I'd almost let go. I would bring the knife so close to my wrist, but then Papa, somewhere up in heaven, had always stopped me.

I went underwater and closed my eyes tight, praying to the God whom I had cursed moments ago. Maybe if I prayed hard enough, I would be back in Chandigarh, sleeping in my oversized T-shirt on the Mickey Mouse bedsheet. Papa would open the door and I would run up to him and give him a big hug. We would drive to Empire Hotel where we would have a huge breakfast of parathas and pancakes.

Maybe this was all just one long bad dream. I would wake up and it would all be over, my life would be okay.

Parmeet

It wasn't often that I thought about those days in Chandigarh when it all began. I was so lonely and miserable. SP had sent Serena off to college in the US and I didn't really get along with the other officers' wives. They were all so svelte and polished, they'd gone to boarding school at Simla and then studied literature at Lady Shri Ram College. They spoke English flawlessly and had afternoon kitty parties at the Gymkhana where they came dressed in chiffon saris and pearl necklaces. They nibbled on cucumber sandwiches and discussed politics, books and the best foreign universities for their children. I didn't fit in with them. My English wasn't very good, I preferred speaking in Punjabi or Hindi. SP had tried to help, he made it a rule that we would only speak in English to each other, but I was too self-conscious. When SP was posted in England, he had hoped that I would pick up the language. He had gently assured me time and again that it was never too late to learn, that one was never too old to change. But even in London I had found my comfort zone in a group of Punjabi housewives. These women were proud to speak in Punjabi. Their English was perfect, they even had an accent, yet they chose to speak in Punjabi and keep their traditions alive.

But language wasn't the only barrier between SP's colleagues' wives and me. I loved bright colours and prints, I didn't own anything that was white or a pastel shade. My mother had drilled it into me that white was a widow's colour. I loved yellow, orange, red, green, I loved sequins and glitter, I loved wearing bright pink lipstick that highlighted my fair skin. I hated the tight churidars that were in vogue and preferred wearing the Patiala salwars I had worn all my life. I hated cucumber sandwiches, they were so bland when compared to piping hot pakoras with chutney and cups of sweet chai or a big glass of lassi.

Once Serena left I realized how empty my life was. SP was always on tour and when I complained to him, he lovingly told me that it was part of his job. He wasn't a junior officer any more, he had major responsibilities as he held a very powerful post. He reminded me about the perks we enjoyed because of his position—the big house, the fleet of cars and the staff. Even though he said it came at a cost, he had to work very hard for it all, I knew he enjoyed the power he wielded. He thought of me as silly old Parmeet, a simple village girl from Punjab, who didn't understand the nuances of his work. I resented him for thinking of me in that light. I felt trapped in the miserable life he had conned me into.

It was around then that I started chatting online. Serena had taught me how to use the Internet, and we often wrote emails to each other. I had heard about chatrooms on TV and out of sheer boredom I decided to see what they were like. I was surprised to find one for people in Chandigarh—'Friends in Chandi'.

Sukdev Singh was twenty-six years old, a little older than Serena. His first question to me was 'I am looking for love, what are you searching for?' I was taken aback. He then sent me a photograph of himself. He was wearing a tight black T-shirt and sunglasses and was standing next to a motorcycle.

Even though the picture was hazy I could make out he was handsome. For some strange reason I found myself aroused. I was so shocked by my reaction that I immediately logged off.

When I went online again the next day he asked me for my photograph. I told him I didn't have one. We then started talking. I confessed that I was much older, but it didn't seem to bother him. We were soon chatting for hours every day. Sukdev was funny and intelligent and he wasn't sophisticated like the other people I knew.

About a week after we started chatting he suggested that we meet. I didn't think about it much. I was glad I had someone who spoke like me and understood where I came from. I was eager to meet my new friend so I agreed to see him. The first thing that struck me was he was very good looking and young. He worked in a music shop where he sold CDs and DVDs. He said he was training to be a DJ. Initially he was surprised to see how old I was, but he hid it well. He flirted with me and repeatedly told me I was beautiful. It felt nice, it had been so long since anyone had complimented me. I invited him home and he was shocked to see the big house and the cars topped with red lights.

I think he was excited by it all—the fact that I was an older woman with a powerful husband.

As for me, I was thrilled, I felt like a young girl again. I found myself jumping out of bed in the morning, wearing the bright, colourful outfits that I loved. I sprayed perfume and put flowers in my hair. I hadn't felt this way since my college days. The time I spent with Sukdev was rejuvenating and, in many ways, therapeutic. I could forget that I led a mundane life, that I had a husband and a grown-up daughter. I felt revived. I loved being the centre of attention, I loved the look of awe in Sukdev's bright young eyes, and I loved the fact that with him I could be whoever I wanted to be—the sexy seductress or the shy bride.

I started dreading the evenings when SP would come home. Couldn't he tell that I didn't care about state politics or the Dhingras' new car? I would sit with him while he drank his tea and wistfully think of the afternoons that I spent with Sukdev. Oh, how young, fresh and handsome he was! He made me feel sixteen again.

One afternoon Sukdev and I had sex. It was inevitable. The attraction had been building up for a while and I knew I couldn't wait any longer so I chose a day when SP was away on a business trip. I dismissed the servants and then invited Sukdev over.

It was wonderful. He was a strong, passionate lover and he kept telling me how beautiful I was. He said he loved my smooth skin, and that I was amazing in bed, unlike his previous girlfriends who would cry out in pain and then kick him off. I held his supple body close to mine as he told me all this. For the first time in years I felt wanted.

However foolish my relationship with Sukdev was, it prepared for me the risk and danger and the glorious rewards of loving Randeep.

I first met Randeep at his clinic. Dr Randeep Singh was recommended by SP's colleague. He had been trained in Delhi, and was young and very bright. SP was impressed with him, he was gentle, calm and professional. For me, it wasn't love at first sight, in fact I had hardly noticed him—I was completely preoccupied with the gall bladder pain.

Dr Randeep performed an emergency surgery on me and I noticed him for the first time only after the operation. I remember thinking I really liked the way his hands felt—soft, stable and firm. I liked how he was always so calm, unlike SP who was chaotic and always in a hurry. Randeep took good care of me, making jokes to ease my worries, touching me tenderly, trying his best not to cause pain while he examined me. I could tell by the way he looked at me, the way he touched me, that he really cared.

My recuperation took longer than expected and I was in that dreary hospital for close to three weeks. It was during that time that I found myself falling in love with Randeep. Sukdev was a distant memory, I hadn't spoken to him or seen him in weeks, and SP's trips to the hospital became less frequent. I found myself keenly waiting for the times when the doctor would come see me, I found myself trying to look as nice as I possibly could in a hospital gown, applying make-up and perfume, doing my hair differently every day. When Randeep touched me now I felt a kind of lightning run through my body, I felt like I had never felt before. It was then that I knew, deep down in my gut, that my life was about to change.

Randeep

The fight with Serena had brought back all those memories that I kept buried. The lying, deceit, fear—I didn't like recalling any of it. But before the terror there was a time when my life was filled with excitement and passion.

As soon as I laid my eyes on Parmeet I knew I was done for. There was something about her that I couldn't resist. It was obvious she was beautiful, even though she was older than me, but there was more to her than just a pretty face. It was in her eyes—they had a fire, a glow that I had never seen before. It was as if I was hit by a bolt of lightning. I was immediately drawn to her, and I got the feeling that she felt the same attraction. Why else would she hold my hand for a second longer than necessary?

We continued to see each when she left the hospital. After all it was procedure for patients to keep in touch with their doctors. We met at my tiny clinic. She would enter and sit across a rickety brown table till I would ask her to lie on the tattered hospital bed covered in white wax paper. I would reach down with the stethoscope and check her heart rate, holding her tiny, fair wrist in my hand, a wrist so delicate that I feared it would snap if I held it too tight. Her hands were breathtaking, I'd never seen any like them, so delicate and beautiful, adorned with golden kaddas and bangles that matched her colourful salwaar kameez.

Often I would keep her by my side for longer than I had to, unnecessarily examining parts of her body, checking her for every disease in the book. Time would pass by so quickly when we were together. I'd keep patients waiting outside the closed door till the peon would enter, pleading. At this point Parmeet would hurriedly leave, fixing the wisps of hair that had come loose from her braid, throwing me a bewitching smile on her way out.

One winter morning I bent forward, stethoscope in hand, holding Parmeet's fragile wrist, taking in her beautiful jasmine scent, listening to her heart beat faster, perfectly in sync with mine, when she whispered in my ear, a soft, seductive whisper that made the hair on my arms stand, 'Doctorji, I don't like the smell of a hospital. It makes me feel like a sick person. Could we meet at my home?'

I agreed, I had been amused by her forward behaviour—no longer was she the frail, shy patient. She was a powerful memsahib who commanded the servants with authority and walked with confidence. We started meeting frequently, far more often than we should have. I, who was proud of my self-control, found that I had lost all sense of reason when it came to her. The time I spent with her was precious and I wished I didn't have to leave her. I wished we could indulge in these dreamy afternoons for the rest of eternity. I lived my life in a daze, I thought of her all the time. Being a doctor I was usually cautious, but with Parmeet I threw caution to the winds. I didn't worry about her husband or her past, I didn't even worry about our future. For the first time in my life I lived for the present—I lived for her, I lived for us.

The day is vivid in my memory and no matter how often I replay it, it is always as wonderful as the first time. SP was out of town, the staff had been dismissed—all except for Sitaram, who Parmeet assured me could be trusted—and we were walking in her beautiful lawn, surrounded by dahlia and roses in bloom. I tried picking a rose for Parmeet and ended up pricking my finger. She had taken my bleeding finger into her mouth and nursed it. She then looked at me with those eyes that could speak with the innocence of a newborn child or preach with the wisdom of a sage. She asked me, as casually as if she were asking whether I wanted tea, if I would like to spend the night with her. I had laughed in an attempt to conceal my surprise because I didn't know what to say. If only she knew how nervous and excited I was. She asked me again and I blushed.

We made love for the first time that night. She was confident and experienced, I was unsteady, nervous and shy but I was overcome by a sense of passion and desire that I had never known before. I hadn't experienced pleasure of this magnitude before. I held her in my arms as she slept, stroking her beautiful face, holding her delicate wrists, and I was overwhelmed with new sensations. It should have terrified me, but I wasn't scared.

With each day I fell deeper in love with her. My sane, rational self told me to forget about her—she was married with a grown-up daughter.

SP was a powerful man. Who knew what he would do if he ever found out. But for once I was able to completely ignore my rational self. I don't know what gave me the courage—maybe it was the thrill of adventure, maybe it was insanity, maybe it was all the poetry that I read, or maybe it was love. Poets have always said that love is irrational and blind, that love knows no boundaries. I was experiencing this in a way that I had never imagined. The odds were against us, but a love this pure, this beautiful, had to survive.

S.P. Sharma's Journal

I loved her from the minute I saw her at Dayal Singh Women's College. I still think of her as I saw her then—her long black hair plaited, with rebellious wisps creating a halo around her face that was flushed pink in the searing heat. Her eyes were aglow with fury as she led a protest against the corrupt principal. She had managed to create quite a stir and I was summoned to end the chaos.

I found it all very amusing as I drove my jeep into the crowd, dispersing them. The girls all ran away screaming, fearing being run over. All save one—Parmeet. She didn't budge from her spot and instead looked straight into my laughing eyes. The grin was wiped off my face and when

I looked back at her rage-filled gaze I knew I was in love.

Our wedding day was the happiest day of my life—I could finally call her my wife. But even then, despite the happiness and euphoria, I sensed, somewhere deep inside, that though we belonged to one another legally, she was never really mine.

Parmeet had always considered herself a class above me. Her father was a wealthy landowner in Ludhiana, whereas both my parents were professors at the Aligarh University. Parmeet despised me in the beginning because I was hell bent on marrying her. She was a real beauty in those days and she had many suitors and even though my career as a police officer was on the rise and accorded me a lot of power, I would never have the kind of wealth that Parmeet was used to. She, like a good Indian girl, left the decision of her marriage to her parents. They found her many suitable men and

she was engaged twice, but each time
I intervened and managed to break the
match. I was young, arrogant and powerful
as the deputy inspector general of police
in Ludhiana, and I had the city under
my control. Her parents finally agreed
to our union because no one would marry
a girl who had two broken engagements.
They would have preferred a wealthy
landowner, someone from their class and
community, but they had to settle for me,
they weren't left with an option. They
reassured their young, nervous seventeen-
year-old daughter that I was powerful
and successful and with time life with
me would improve.

I gave her everything she wanted—she
only had to name it and it was hers. More
than anything else, I gave her all my
love. I worked like a dog to provide her
and Serena a good life and this is how
she repays me.

At first I didn't believe the rumours. I
thought the other women were jealous—why

else would they say such awful things about my wife? But after a while I couldn't ignore them any more. I'd enter the clubroom and everyone would fall silent. I'd see my juniors smirking behind my back. The whole town was talking about Parmeet's infidelity. I had become a laughing stock. People spoke about how they had seen her with some guy called Sukdev, and now there was Dr Randeep. I still didn't believe them, but I had to know for sure. So I had Sukdev brought to the police station where I beat a confession out of him.

I have been in the police service for over twenty-five years. I can smell trouble, and I know when I am being lied to. And now that I have proof, I see signs everywhere. She speaks for hours on the phone late at night saying she is talking to Serena in America, but the laughter and the whispers I overhear suggest otherwise. I often see her writing letters and when I inquire she says they are for

Serena, 'girl talk', she says with a sweet smile. It all makes sense now—she moved out of our bedroom after her operation saying she needed time to heal. Months later when I suggested she move back she said she slept better now without my snoring to keep her awake. Of course she needs her own bedroom, she wouldn't dare sleep with that doctor in my bed.

Parmeet is oblivious, she doesn't realize that I suspect her of cheating on me. And if the signs weren't evident I wouldn't believe it myself. But when I see her looking youthful and brighter every time I return from a trip out of town, I don't have a doubt.

My work is beginning to suffer, I can think of nothing else but Parmeet's affairs. I can't get the picture of her with another man out of my mind, I have become obsessive. I have started drinking heavily and smoking, I find it is the only way I can calm down. I am usually so calm and gentle with her, but I find myself questioning her like I do suspects and petty theives. She denies everything. She never loses her calm, she never sheds a tear. She just shakes her head and looks at me with contempt in her eyes, those very same eyes that I love so much. I can't understand how I still love her when I hate her so much.

Randeep

Once I started remembering the past, I couldn't stop the memories. I still feel sick when I think about SP's persecution. The man was on a mission to destroy my life. He sent his goons to the clinic to threaten my patients and ruin my practice. They even came to my house one day and beat me up. I realized I wasn't safe in Chandigarh any more. I was scared for my life, but more importantly I was scared for Parmeet. I had to leave town for a while.

I decided to move to Delhi where my parents lived, hoping that time with my family would give me some perspective and help me forget the passion that I felt for Parmeet. She wept when I told her about my decision, she begged me not to go. I promised her I would be back, but at that moment we both needed to sort out the complexities in our lives. She was married with a child—it was her dharma to tend to her family. And I strongly believed that the purity of our love would draw us together again in the future. She took a deep breath, wiped her tears and smiled weakly. She knew she needed to get her life back on track. Feigning strength, I told her she couldn't just throw away her life for passion, though inwardly I wept at the thought of being away from her.

Parmeet

My life was perfect now, except for Serena who could be very difficult at times. But things weren't always like this. There was a time when I thought I was living in hell and I'd never get out. SP forced Randeep to leave Chandigarh and then turned his vengeance on me. He still expected me to accompany him to official parties, but at home he acted like I didn't exist. Those were the darkest days of my life. I felt like I had nothing to live for any more. Serena was in another country and she didn't know about what was happening at home. She was having a tough time with Salman and I didn't want to burden her with my troubles. I missed Randeep terribly. There were days when I would lie in bed till the evening because there was nothing to wake up for, there was nothing to look forward to. The time that I had spent with Randeep faded into a dream, and in my darkest moments I sometimes wondered if he was even real. I was slowly falling down a deep abyss and there was nothing I could do to stop myself.

It was then that I met Jaspal Dhingra. SP had dragged me to a state dinner where I spent the evening alone in a corner. Everyone knew my husband detested me and no one wanted to anger him by even talking to me. SP was in a good mood tonight socializing with his colleagues. Their wives were all dressed in silk saris and expensive jewellery and they were chatting gaily while they occasionally cast furtive glances at me.

I was embarrassed and was waiting for the evening to end when Jaspal Dhingra walked over and started talking to me. Jaspal Dhingra was an industrialist who was infamous for his philandering ways. He apparently enjoyed the company of young foreign women and regularly entertained them at one of the many hotels he owned around town. I couldn't understand why he chose to speak to me, I was hardly his type. But, surprisingly, I enjoyed talking to him. There was something dashing and noble about Jaspal—he was such a charmer. He looked good in his imposing red turban which matched the pocket square tucked neatly into his black bandhgala. His snow-white beard was neatly trimmed, and the curl in his long moustache was perfectly waxed. Before the evening was over, he slipped me his card and whispered that he would call me soon.

Over the next few weeks Jaspal and I became friends. He was a gentleman and time passed quickly when I was with him. We didn't have much in common, but somehow we always found things to talk about. He was funny and made me laugh and I was impressed that he wasn't afraid of SP. But soon I got the feeling that Jaspal was falling in love with me. I was flattered, of course. I even toyed with the idea of sleeping with him, but every time I thought about it, I pictured Randeep's face. That's when I knew I was hopelessly in love with Randeep. SP thought Randeep and my relationship was only about sex, but there was so much more to it, though I couldn't let him get a whiff of it. I knew he wouldn't hesitate in killing Randeep if he knew we were in love. He could be quite ruthless when he wanted. So I pretended to flirt with Jaspal to divert SP's attention away from Randeep.

Jaspal had recently started a chain of schools across Punjab, and he offered me the principal's job at the school in Chandigarh. He said I was perfect for it, college educated, street-smart, and the wife of a senior bureaucrat. I didn't think I was up to it, after all my English was terrible, but he reassured me that it would improve with time. I was still hesitant about accepting his offer—I hadn't worked a day in my life. Would I be able to deal with it? Surprisingly, SP encouraged this step, he said it would keep me busy. He then started emotionally blackmailing me, saying it was a credible profession for an officer's wife and I needed the job to help clean up my reputation and kill the gossip.

Once I got the hang of things I found I enjoyed the job immensely. I loved the feeling of control and authority and enjoyed having people look up to me and treat me with respect, especially after being gossiped about. Having spent so many years married to an administrative leader, I felt I had already experienced second-hand the many pitfalls of running an organization and I found myself well prepared for the challenges that I faced. I had never felt so content, and by focusing all my energies on the school I was able to keep my mind off Randeep.

S.P. Sharma's Journal

The day I married Parmeet I had vowed to stop drinking and smoking. It was my wedding present to her. But now every promise that we had made on that sacred day has been broken. I sit in my study and smoke cigarette after cigarette while finishing off bottles of single malt.

I don't see much of Parmeet these days. She leaves for school early in the morning and when I come home from work, she is already in bed. I don't sleep a lot, most nights I stay up late drinking. I prefer to drink alone though there are invitations from friends. I don't want them to know how pathetic my life is. I pour my whisky on the rocks and lose myself in thought. I often find myself thinking of Serena. I worry about her. I see so much of myself in her. Like me she is strong yet weak when it comes to those she loves. She portrays herself as confident, but her insecurities are just lurking below the surface. I wish that one day she finds the kind of strength her mother has. I can't deny it—Parmeet might be turning my life upside down, but she is strong. She doesn't crack under pressure.

My darling Serena is so young. Parmeet and I have taken a conscious decision not to let on about our troubles. Serena has enough to worry about as it is. She is having problems with that Muslim boy. I knew he was not good enough for her! But she is so far away, all alone in a foreign land, and she is no longer a child . . . what can I possibly do?

I am up every night worrying about my marriage, my daughter, and I have no one to turn to. I miss the old days when we were a family. We were so happy. How has it all come to this?

Serena

Amar, Amar, Amar—he was all I could think about
today. His name echoed loudly through my head.
There was no sound to distract me. The house was
silent. It made me nervous, I wasn't used to this. I
couldn't hear the baby crying, or Ma screaming at
Ramu, even the TV was off. Then I remembered
that everybody had gone to Chandigarh for the
weekend, and I relaxed a little bit. I lit a cigarette
and took a long drag. My morning cigarette was
perhaps the most peaceful part of my day.

I don't know why I missed him so much today.
I thought of the night when we first met—New
Year's Eve. It was my first month in Delhi, and I
didn't know many people. I was at a big New Year's
party at Zenith, the hippest club in Delhi. A few
acquaintances from New York had invited me and
I was in no mood to sit at home with Ma and

Randeep, so I went. Despite the cold I wore a short backless fuschia dress. My mother even allowed me to wear her long, dangly diamond earrings.

I was having a great time dancing when one of my friends brought him to my notice. Looking handsome in a dark blazer, a pink tie and pink socks, he couldn't take his eyes off me. Our eyes met for a fleeting second, he winked at me and I shyly looked away. We danced later, very briefly, his arms around my waist, his fingers brushing my bare back.

Oh, what a night it was. I still feel giddy thinking about it. The club was rocking, the music loud, the champagne popping. When I left shortly after sunrise, he asked me for my number. He then kissed me on the cheek and said goodbye. It was only when we were in the car did my friends tell me who he was—Amar Khanna, son of an industrialist and married into one of Delhi's richest families.

For the next few days all I could think of was him. I knew he was married, but for some reason that didn't bother me, I still wanted him. I didn't hear from Amar for an entire week. I had given up hope when I ran into him at Khan Market. He apologized profusely for not calling, complaining of a hectic travel schedule. He asked me to have coffee with him. He had looked so cute with a white scarf tied around his neck, the tip of his perfect nose rosy in the chill. I couldn't resist. He called me that night and asked me out for a drink. I desperately wanted to see him, but I told him, with practised nonchalance, that I was busy that evening.

When I didn't hear from him for another week I was afraid my ploy to play hard to get had backfired. But he did call me a few days later and I was so happy I agreed to meet him immediately. I wouldn't have missed it for the world. He came to pick me up in a black Mercedes-Benz with a uniformed chauffeur and a personal security officer. Having a PSO was the latest thing in Delhi those days.

We went to his friend's house where there were a few other couples. They were all older than me and were obviously very rich. But they were also friendly and after my third Jack Daniel's and coke, I found myself having a great time. The night was a dream and I didn't want it to end. Amar was a perfect gentleman, he was by my side the entire evening, introducing me to all his friends. Even when he was talking to other people, I could feel his eyes on me.

The party wrapped up at around two in the morning. I grudgingly said goodbye, not knowing when I would meet Amar next. As I stared out of the car window, I felt him reach for my hand.

'Darling, you aren't going anywhere yet. I want to take you to a special place,' he said.

I was elated and I couldn't stop smiling as we drove to Gurgaon. I wasn't familiar with the area, so I stopped trying to figure out where we were going and I focussed on memorizing Amar's face instead. The driver parked the car outside a recently built skyscraper. Amar led me past a pile of rubble to an opulent lobby with marble flooring and a big crystal chandelier. We then rode the elevator to the penthouse. It was a large, beautiful apartment that smelt of fresh paint. Amar took me on a tour—six bedrooms, eight bathrooms and the largest terrace I had ever seen. The shiny marble floors were dazzling, as were the gold fittings in the bathrooms. We walked through the French windows that led out to the terrace. Amar held my hand as we leaned against the railing, looking out at the city. We were so high up that all we could see were twinkling lights everywhere. Amar turned me to face him, holding my chin, his other hand against the small of my back.

'Worth the trip?' he asked in a raspy whisper.

I smiled and nodded. He then gently brought his face towards mine and kissed me. I felt my red lipstick rub off on his lips.

The next night we met at his company guest house. We had wild, passionate sex. And that was just the beginning.

We met night after night and each time the sex got better. I came to know the intricacies of his body, what made his back arch, where the soft tufts of hair were the densest, when his muscles tensed. I learnt where he liked being touched, the positions he enjoyed and the exact moment when he would come. He loved exploring my body, finding the place where my skin was the softest, running his fingers down the curve where my waist gave way to my voluptuous hips and each time his touch made me shudder.

We always did Charlie. It was normal for him, for me it was a new experience. I had tried it a couple of times in New York and I didn't like the feeling too much, in fact it had been a total let-down. People had told me that Charlie made you rock all night, but I didn't feel that way at all. I would just rather get drunk. But with Amar, cocaine was different. With him it was absolutely, unbelievably, incredibly amazing! And sex after coke was the best ever. I enjoyed every caress, every movement, every thrust much more, I could feel everything deep inside me. Amar would rub cocaine on my body, in places that I had never imagined, and it felt like I was being touched for the first time. I could feel the intensity of each caress, the sensuality of each movement. I had had great sex before, but this was something else, it was stronger, deeper, divine.

After we had exhausted ourselves we would spend the rest of the night talking. Well, he would talk and I'd listen. Most of what he said was coked-out nonsense. I would lie in the nook of his arm and he'd twirl a strand of my hair, round and round, while he went on about nothing in particular. I never could remember exactly what he spoke about, he was coked out and so was I. A sense of happiness enveloped me, and I had not felt this way for a very long time.

I saw him enter the club and my heart skipped a beat. I felt that crazy rush of excitement, nervousness and anxiety rise through my body like lightning, making me feel giddy.

I was at the bar with friends when he walked in, followed by her. Even though I didn't know what she looked like I immediately knew it was her. There was this chemistry between them. They weren't even holding hands or anything but it was evident they were married. I have to admit, Preiti Khanna was attractive. She wasn't beautiful by any means, but she had lovely fair skin, delicate feminine features and soft, chocolate-coloured eyes. She wore minimal make-up and was dressed in white trousers and an expensive beige coat. With a sinking feeling, I realized that she was a picture of perfection—pretty, kind and happy. Seeing Preiti my confidence vanished and suddenly I felt unattractive, ugly—compared to her my make-up was too dark, the colour of my hair too bright, my clothes cheap and my body fat. Why would someone like Amar choose me? How on earth did he find me attractive? I felt like total shit, I just wanted another drink and I wanted to forget about him forever.

I saw Amar walking towards me, he politely said hello to my friends and gave me a friendly hug and a kiss on each cheek. Before he returned to his wife he came close to me and whispered in my ear, his lips brushing lightly against my ear lobe, 'You look very beautiful tonight.'

I knew he'd call me later and he did—at 7.12 a.m. I was asleep and at first I thought it was a dream, but the phone kept ringing. I didn't even bother opening my eyes to look at the number flashing on the screen, I just knew it was Amar.

'Serena?' Even in that drowsy state my heart did a flip-flop. 'Beautiful, I want to see you,' he said in that fabulous voice of his, made huskier by the cigarettes and alcohol.

'Amar . . .' I was still so sleepy I could barely say his name.

'Darling, listen, I need to see you,' he said urgently.

I was wide awake now. 'What do you want?' I croaked.

'You know what I want, beautiful,' he laughed. 'Sweetie, you know exactly what I want . . . I want you.'

'It's seven in the morning, Amar. I can't meet you right now.' I was still upset about seeing him with Preiti last night.

'Darling, please don't do this to me right now. I am absolutely dying to see you. I would do anything to be with you. Tell me what I can do to change your mind.'

The fervour in his voice, that tone, it stirred something inside me. I wanted to be with him too, so badly. But I knew it wasn't right to see him now, he was totally coked out. I could hear it in his voice.

'Sweetie, please?' he asked desperately.

I closed my eyes, my body ached for him, but my brain told me otherwise. It was 7 fucking a.m. I had to say no, for his sake and mine. Amar was an addiction, far worse than cigarettes or any other drug. He was married! I had seen him with his wife yesterday. I had to fight the urge.

'No, Amar. Not today,' I said, trying to sound emphatic, though I ached for him. I winced as I heard him hang up on me.

It had been a month since Amar had called. He said he'd been away on business and had missed me terribly. It was six in the morning, but I couldn't resist, I had gone for too long without him. I did my make-up in a hurry and tied my greasy, limp hair in a ponytail. In my haste I couldn't find sexy underwear, so I didn't wear any at all.

He was waiting for me at the door to his guest house. As I got out of the car he walked towards me with an exaggerated swagger. He grabbed me by my waist and kissed me more passionately than usual. I could feel the frenzy in his kiss and I gently pushed him away.

'Amar, how are you?' I asked with a nervous smile. 'I haven't heard from you in a while.'

'Baby, you look so hot,' he replied. 'Do you have any idea how much I've missed you?'

'Did you really now, Mr Khanna?' I asked trying to sound sexy, though I didn't really feel it.

'Oh, baby, if you only knew,' he said, drawing me closer.

I just laughed and pushed him away again. 'Amar, you're being so naughty! I want to talk to you. I want to hear about your trip.'

He took a deep breath, and then exhaled. He looked a little annoyed. 'Babe, it was all good— Rome, London, Paris. There was only one thing missing.'

'What was that?' I asked trying to sound coy.

'You, baby.' Again he pulled me close, this time kissing me insistently. Why was he behaving like this today? He usually wasn't so forceful, he liked taking things nice and slow.

As soon as we were indoors he reached for the waistband of my sweatpants and pulled them down. I stopped his hand as he reached for me. 'Amar, I'm not in the mood.'

He stepped away and smiled. Then he kissed my forehead. 'Sugar, we'll get you in the mood.'

He pulled out a small vial and a credit card from his pocket and placed them on the table. 'Sweet, sweet sugar,' he said with a gleeful laugh.

He cut ten lines and handed me a pipe made from a thousand-rupee note. I did five lines and didn't even wince. As the coke started hitting me I realized that Amar was blown. I could see his pupils dilate and the slight shivers that cocaine always gave him.

He stood up and went to the refrigerator and took out two cans of beer, handing one to me. 'Breakfast,' he said with a wink. Just as I opened my can, he pulled it out of my hands and put it on the table. 'Dance with me,' he said, even though there was no music playing.

I laughed nervously, I could feel the cocaine now and I didn't like the way my body was reacting to it. That was the thing with cocaine, sometimes it felt amazing, but sometimes it made me feel so terrible, really nervous and anxious. I felt beads of perspiration break out on my upper lip. I wanted this feeling to go away.

Amar shoved his hands up my top. I allowed him to this time. I just closed my eyes and tried thinking sexy thoughts. I tried concentrating on him, I took a deep breath and took in his perfume—a mix of musk, smoke and alcohol. I reached for his belt buckle as he reached down to touch me. I felt myself stiffen and step back. What had come over me? I was never like this. I felt nervous, almost scared of Amar. I opened my eyes and looked at him. His face was strangely contorted, he was breathing heavily and staring at me.

'What's wrong, baby?' he asked gently, stroking my hair.

'I . . . I don't know, babe, I just feel weird. Is it okay if we just talk?'

He looked at me, up and down, and pulled me close again. He gently bit my ear and whispered, 'But, baby, I've missed you.'

'I know, sweetheart, I've missed you too,' I replied, not sounding very convincing. I wriggled out of his grasp as nicely as I could. My head was spinning, I was sweating profusely and I was starting to feel nauseous.

'Amar,' I said, wiping the sweat away with my T-shirt, 'baby, I need to go home.'

'Sweets, c'mon!' He grabbed my waist, one hand reaching to undo his jeans.

I squirmed in his strong grasp. 'Amar, baby, please no,' I said trying my best to sound light and cheery, though I felt like crying. What the hell was wrong with me today? I wanted him so badly all this while so why was I feeling this way now? 'Amar, I need to go home. Baby, I'll see you later tonight, okay?'

For a few seconds we stood as we were, Amar's hands around my hips, my body tense and uncomfortable. He looked into my eyes, and I felt scared, his pupils were dilated and his face was pale.

Suddenly he let go of me. 'Fine,' he said. 'Go, go home.'

I pulled up my pants from where they were bunched at my knees and, grabbing my bag, I walked away quickly. I didn't even turn back to blow him a kiss.

The heat outside felt good against my skin. It soaked through my top, giving me warmth. I put on my sunglasses and started the car. I drove home slowly, smoking a cigarette. I looked at myself in the mirror while I waited at a red light. My face was puffy, my smudged kajal had left black streaks all over, my hair was a total mess. My body ached and my tummy felt numb. I was sweating even though the AC was on. I wanted this feeling to stop, this terrible panicky feeling after cocaine. Slowly the tears started coming and then they wouldn't stop. I wanted these feelings to disappear, I just wanted to go home and for all of this to be over.

Parmeet

I remember the day he came back to me. It was a rainy Sunday afternoon. I was in the veranda sipping a cup of sweet tea and eating crisp pakoras while watching the rain come down washing away all the dust and grime of the summer. SP was on tour that weekend and I was enjoying the freedom.

The phone rang, and I answered. He told me softly, in Punjabi, that he was back in Chandigarh and that he wanted to see me. He didn't say anything else. Just when I had begun to wake up every morning without feeling a deep sense of loss, without thinking of him, without craving him, he had come back.

Half an hour later I opened the door and there he was. We just stood there for several minutes looking at each other because neither one of us could believe this was real. The very second I laid eyes on him, all the old feelings returned, stronger than ever before. It was as if he had never left, as if he had been by my side all this time.

It was a little awkward initially because we were both so nervous, and I was not used to such feelings. I didn't know what to say or how to behave. We sat in the living room across from each other like a young, shy couple, too nervous to look directly at each other. We just stared at the untouched cups of tea that lay in front of us letting the joy sink in.

We were jolted out of our trance-like state when I heard the front door open loudly and the sound of SP's footsteps echoed down the hallway towards the living room.

S.P. Sharma's Journal

I was livid. I knew the hatred and vengeance I felt were clearly visible in my eyes. Something inside me snapped when I saw them sitting across each other, their eyes speaking volumes. I have to get rid of her, it is now a matter of my pride. I stormed out of the room and went to my library where I prepared a stiff drink for myself. I didn't sleep that night, I couldn't. Instead I drank and smoked and schemed. I believed that her job at the school would rid her of her vices, but instead it has brought out the devil in her. I have been hearing things, nasty things, about Jaspal Dhingra and the woman I called my wife—rumours that make my blood boil, and now the brute doctor is back. I'll show these men what it means to mess with S.P. Sharma, and this woman, this swine, I have to set her right, I absolutely have to get my dignity back.

Parmeet

I remember that morning like it was yesterday, that terrible, terrible morning when all hell broke loose. I came down to find that dirty man in the same clothes he was wearing last night, reeking of alcohol and smoke. I was at the door leaving for school when he came towards me and said in a voice empty of all emotion, 'You're not going to school today, you are going to quit your job.'

I just laughed at him, thinking he had really lost his mind. I started walking out when he suddenly grabbed my hair and pulled me towards him, his face so close to mine I could smell his sour breath. I screamed in pain, but none of the servants even dared to look. Sitaram, unfortunately, wasn't there. SP told me, without raising his voice which was now seething with contempt, 'Memsahib, your precious school is being shut down, and Dhingra, that harami, your chootiya lover is going to jail. If you dare step out of this house I'll break your legs.' He then pushed me towards the stairs, and I ran up to my bedroom and bolted the door, too scared to even shed a tear.

I spent the next few days cooped up in my room, I was petrified that SP would break in and beat me or even kill me. That monster was capable of anything in this state of mind. Fear did not allow me to sleep. I could see the shadow of his feet near the door. He stood there for several hours while I lay in bed frozen, chanting the Lord's name. There was no one who could help me, no one I could confide in. I desperately wanted to contact Randeep, to escape this hell and go somewhere far, far away with him, but I knew that would only make things worse. Something inside me screamed and I knew that Randeep was in trouble. I had to warn him. SP wielded the power of the corrupt Punjab police and he could put anyone behind bars, I had seen him do it before. I scribbled a note to Randeep asking him to leave town immediately and sent my faithful servant Sitaram to deliver it. I desperately hoped that the note would reach him in time, and that he would heed my warning and leave town.

Over the next few days the terror unfolded in front of my eyes. The life I had built for myself collapsed without a whisper, like a fragile house of cards. The school was taken over by the police and Jaspal Dhingra, along with several of my colleagues, was arrested for the possession and distribution of drugs. They accused Jaspal of financing the school with black money acquired from underworld connections, and as simply as that the school was shut down, a big lock placed on its gates, all the teachers and staff without jobs, the children deprived of their education.

SP made me visit Jaspal in jail. He was so sadistic. He said he wanted me to see the extent of his power. I could hardly recognize the man they brought in front of me. In just a matter of days, the fine, noble Jaspal Dhingra, who was always groomed to the finest, appeared to have aged decades and had been reduced to skin and bones. Scars covered his body. The fragile, old man wept in front of me.

He held my hands in his shaking, coarse hands. 'Why is this happening to me?' he asked not expecting an answer. 'What have I done?' He told me they beat him every day in a cell that reeked of death. They wanted him to confess to adultery. He didn't let go of my hands the entire time I was there and he didn't stop crying, the once-powerful, charismatic Jaspal Dhingra. He told me over and over again that he would never admit to committing adultery.

I wanted to cry but I had no tears left. I was so tortured and tormented myself that I found I was incapable of feeling. Before I left I told him to have faith in God, though I didn't have much left myself.

SP had turned into a jealous demon who plotted and schemed to tear apart the small, happy life that I had created for myself. He was a powerful man in Punjab and commanded a great deal of respect, he had done favours for a lot of people and he reaped the benefits now.

He told me he wanted a divorce. Just a week ago I would have welcomed it, I had often thought of suggesting it myself, but now, with the school gone and with Jaspal in jail, I had no one to turn to, nowhere to go. Also, I feared for Randeep, that poor, powerless soul. I was sure SP would kill Randeep if I went to him. I wept, I begged, for Serena's sake, I said, she was so young, it wasn't right to do this to her. But he just ignored me like one does a beggar. That bastard, he wouldn't budge. He was intent on destroying me.

Randeep

I knew it was a mistake to return to Chandigarh, but the entire time I was away from Parmeet I couldn't stop thinking about her. I longed for the warmth of her soft body, her loud laughter, her bright clothes. I had a hard time reminding myself that I was doing this for her good. In the end I caved, and SP caught us. I knew I had to leave Chandigarh again, this time for good. I got her note, it had been slipped under my door at night. My first instinct was to rescue her from that demon, how could I possibly abandon the person I loved the most in this world and care for my own safety? Who knew what he would do to her. I was anxious with fear and guilt but I knew that if I went to her, he would kill me. I had to leave. I had no other choice.

My modest home was plundered, furniture broken, glass shattered, my few belongings scattered all over the place. I was numb with fear. It was like a terrible dream, these sort of things did not happen to simple men like me. With a heart burning with terror I fled taking with me nothing save the money I had in my wallet. I ran in fear, praying for her life over mine, hoping dearly that I would soon wake up from this nightmare.

Parmeet

SP made me leave. I went to my parents' home in Ludhiana, the only place where I could go. They all looked at me with shame and disgrace in their eyes, a divorced woman deserved a fate worse than death. I, being the youngest child and the only daughter had always been treated like a rajkumari, a princess, but now I was treated like a pariah. I was housed in a room that had previously belonged to the cook, and hardly anyone spoke to me. Ma had told me that a divorced woman was a blemish on the family name and if she hadn't forced my father, he wouldn't have taken me in.

S.P. Sharma's Journal

I threw Parmeet out, but somehow she managed to tip-off Randeep and he had escaped. But I promise myself I will find him and kill him. Through the course of my career I have come to know many powerful people, and I am now using them all to carry out my search—the Punjab mafia, heads of the local Sikh gangs, the Muslim gangs. I have instructed these men to hunt down Randeep Singh; I will make him confess his sins, even if it means torturing him till death.

Randeep

For months after leaving town I lived the life of a fugitive, fleeing from one place to another, staying no longer than a day at each location. I didn't dare contact anyone, not Parmeet, not my family, I didn't want to cause them harm. I only had a few thousand rupees so I had to learn to survive. I lived a life of constant fear, travelling in third class train compartments, spending nights at railway stations and bus stops across Punjab and Haryana—Moga, Ambala, Panipat, Patiala, Nabha, Rohtak—I tried to avoid following a pattern. I had several narrow escapes—at the Rohtak bus station I saw them arrive with lathis and chains just as the bus I was in drove away. At a tea shop in Nabha they attacked with guns as I drove away in a lorry packed with frightened women and children. They almost had me in Hisar where they chased me through a crowded marketplace before I found refuge in a wedding procession. Posters bearing my photograph appeared in the most obscure places and a ransom was placed on my head. I grew a beard and wore a turban hoping to disguise my looks, but everywhere I went I felt like I was being watched. Sleep eluded me and I did not have a minute of rest, a single second of peace. What bothered me most, what kept me awake night after night, was not the fear of losing my life, but the thought of what had happened to Parmeet. I had no news from her, and I remember thinking if only I knew she was safe, if only I knew she was taken care of, I would be at peace, but I had nothing. I desperately wished to speak to her, my soul grieved and my heart ached. I yearned for her. In moments of weakness I would come close to posting the long letters I would write to her.

I realized I had to get my life back, if only for Parmeet's sake, and the only way forward was for me to be powerful in my own right. I had to become a part of SP's system. After months on the run I went to Delhi, back to my parents, and I started studying for the IAS exam. I was determined, my mind focussed on my goal, because I knew it was the only way for me to get my woman and my life back.

Those few months changed my life. Until this point of my existence, I had always been afraid of embarking upon the unknown, and therefore I had chosen the safest, most secure life I knew—the medical profession—because that was what my father had chosen. I found peace and calm in medicine, but not fulfilment. I yearned to experience the kind of power that S.P. Sharma wielded. I, too, wanted to be equipped with that kind of strength. I realized that the only access to that degree of power was through the Indian Administrative Service.

The rite of passage to the intellectual elite was through a difficult and highly competitive examination. Thankfully, taking examinations had always been my forté. I had aced numerous ones to become a doctor, and I was confident of my ability to fare well in this exam too. I studied feverishly for months, going back to all my medical books. Among the millions who took the civil services exam that year, I ranked in the top ten and I proudly became an officer of the bureaucratic elite, the Indian Administrative Service.

My acceptance into the IAS was a passport to my freedom. At long last I was safe from the demonic clutches of S.P. Sharma. Away at the academy in

Mussoorie I was safe, the powers of the IAS on my side. My dearest Parmeet could finally be mine. She had written to me about her divorce and the shameful treatment her family was meting out to her. We were married just before I had to leave for the academy in a small, intimate ceremony in Delhi attended only by my family. On our wedding night we conceived our sweet daughter, our reward for all the struggles that we had had to endure to be with each other.

There was only one thing that had me worried. Parmeet hadn't told Serena about her divorce and our marriage. Her daughter had heard nothing of the drama that had ensued in India because SP had not wanted to trouble her. But I felt it was time Serena knew and I urged Parmeet to tell her. After all, it was inevitable that she would find out about the marriage and the new baby one day.

Riya

Serena often came over when she fought with her parents. I didn't know much about her life, just that her dad had died and her mom was now remarried with a baby. I guess she found some kind of a peace by recounting her stories to me—for her it was a therapeutic process. I hadn't met anyone like her before, someone with a life so utterly tragic that at many times it was almost comical. There were daily mishaps in Serena's life. Ever so often old rickety would break down at the worst of times, and I would wake up in the wee hours of the morning to a call for help. I hated answering her distress calls, but a part of me felt like I owed it to her. For some strange reason I felt like I had to watch out for her, even though we weren't really friends.

Then there were the incessant fights she would have with her mother and stepfather. Often she would be told to leave the house and not return and at those times she would come over to my place. She would talk angrily, but she would never cry, and I would listen to her, and let her rant till she had worked the anger out of her system, settling into a semi-peaceful silence before quietly going back home.

Serena was the closest I had to a friend in Delhi. Even though I went out with her all the time, I hadn't managed to make any friends. A few guys had asked me out on dates and considering how bored I was with my life I would have accepted if they had been even halfway decent, but these men were unimaginably shady. I shiver every time I picture those cretins. One guy introduced himself as Rocky. He wore tight jeans, a thick gold chain, a tight black T-shirt and had hair that shone like a bright penny because of all the gel. Rocky was impressed with my American accent and had asked me out for a champagne dinner at one of the most expensive restaurants in town. I honestly felt that most of these shady guys hit on me because they thought that their chances of getting laid were higher with girls who spoke with an American accent.

My life in Delhi continued down this path. There were always parties to attend and people to meet. I realized that it wasn't difficult for girls in Delhi, especially single girls. It wasn't like in America where even good-looking girls found themselves alone on a Saturday night. Serena and Pinky, though not particularly hot, were invited everywhere—polo matches during the season, weddings, art exhibitions, store openings, wine tastings, book launches. The funny thing was no one really cared about polo or art or books. Most of the time they didn't even know the people hosting the event, but they went because they knew everyone else was going to be there. On a night when there weren't any parties, the social set would turn up at the same restaurants hoping to bump into someone they knew.

What amazed me was that though they hung out together all the time, it didn't stop them from bitching about each other. Serena would tell me about the bitter enmity between two women and the next evening I'd see the same women chatting like long-lost friends. Most of the bitchiness stemmed from extramarital affairs. This group of people was so incestuous—they were all sleeping with each other's husbands and wives. It was all quite crazy. But since I was an outsider it didn't greatly affect my life. I just went with the flow, chilling, with no real purpose or direction, being mildly entertained by Serena's colourful life, hoping that something would happen to me.

'He put one hand on my shoulder and the other around my waist and, looking straight into my eyes, he told me that I was his girl—*his* girl! Isn't that sweet?' squealed Serena, her eyes bright with excitement.

'Was he high?' I asked sceptically.

'No, we didn't do anything. We weren't even in bed. We went for a long drive, and then he parked on the side of a quiet road and we kissed; he kissed me so deeply, it was so romantic,' she said in a dreamy voice. 'He looked really good and he was such a gentleman. What a night! It was like we were kids again—like we were back in school. It was something else—sweet, innocent, amazing. I think I might be falling in love with him,' she said with a sigh. 'Can you believe he said that? "You're my girl," he told me.'

I'd never seen Serena like this before. She seemed happy, cheerful, carefree. On Sunday afternoons she was usually grumpy and moody, a result of the alcohol and drugs from the previous night. But today she was different. Today she was bubbly and silly and giggly, like a schoolgirl. I wanted to tell her to stay away from him. Usually I was the stupidest person with this sort of thing. I didn't know much about relationships and men, but even I knew that Amar Khanna was no good. Serena had blinkers on and she couldn't see what an utter asshole the guy was, treating her like shit, calling her in the middle of the night to see him, making her drive to godforsaken places to meet him. For heaven's sake the man was married. I couldn't understand what she was doing with him. Couldn't she see that this relationship wasn't going anywhere, that he was only in it for the sex? Didn't she realize that loving him was sadistic?

Amar

It was 3 a.m. on a Saturday and we were very high. I was at Mumta and Aveesh's place with Meeru and the four of us were having a great time when she suggested we play strip poker. Halfway through the game only Meeru and I were left playing—the others were too strung out on coke to even think straight so they lay on the couch watching us.

I looked across at Meeru who was laughing sexily. I have to admit I'd never really found her attractive before, but tonight she was looking rather tempting. She had definitely lost weight over the summer, and the red hair colour suited her. Meeru had been giving me the look all evening. I know what it means when a girl looks at you that way. To be honest, I wasn't looking so shabby myself. I was wearing the new shirt I had bought in Italy and the watch Preiti had gifted me looked splendid.

I avoided looking at the time though. It made me nervous—what if Preiti woke up and realized I wasn't home again? I didn't want to deal with any of that crap tonight. We had a big showdown yesterday and she told me if I continued to behave this way, if I didn't stop partying, she would divorce me, leave me with nothing, take away our son and her father's support. It was the same old bullshit every time, she didn't have the guts to divorce me. There was no way in hell she could deal with being called a divorcee, especially now with the baby. I usually called her bluff, but last night I was so damn tired. Her screeching had totally killed my high, so I just shrugged my shoulders and ignored the woman's rants.

'Amar, darling, I have a full house,' said Meeru, bringing me back to the present. 'You know what that means—strip!'

Was it my imagination or did she wink at me? I was down to my shirt and boxers so I decided to make a show of taking off my shirt. I slowly undid each button as I moved to the music, my eyes fixed on Meeru who laughed and then looked away coyly. That woman really knew how to turn a man on. I shrugged out of my shirt and swung it in the air, round and round, in tune to the music. I then threw it on Meeru who shrieked in delight. 'The rest is for your eyes only, darling,' I said. She rolled her eyes and stuck her tongue out at me. Underneath her confident veneer she blushed and I knew I had her.

As I dealt the cards we continued to drink from the bottle of whisky that lay on the table and doing lines from a salt shaker full of cocaine, courtesy me. My phone rang and Serena's picture flashed on the screen. I debated answering the call. Serena Sharma—I thought of her as I had last seen her, dressed in black, heavily made up, her lips a deep red. She wasn't the type of girl I was usually attracted to. I preferred glamorous chicks, but there was something so irresistibly sexy about Serena. She did things to me that I didn't quite understand. She was wild and crazy and free. There weren't many people like her in Delhi, she reminded me so much of my college days in the US—the best days of my life, when I didn't have to worry about anything. No wife, no kid, no fucking society bullshit. I was carefree, irresponsible, spontaneous.

Serena was young, and young girls were usually trouble, but I knew she was different. Serena was somehow older than her twenty-four years. She wasn't timid, shy or stupid like so many other young Indian girls. She was confident, cool and incredible in bed—better than anyone I knew. But the blonde hair, the fake American accent, her plump body, could be a turn-off at times, but I still really liked the way she looked. When I was away from her, I found myself thinking about her—even when I was abroad and there were so many beautiful women around. With Serena it was somehow different. Of course, the sex was amazing, but it wasn't just that. Somehow she understood me, and I had a really fucked-up mind. Unlike most people she didn't expect anything from me. She was happy with just me. With her I didn't have to pretend to be someone I wasn't. I was so sick of it—I had to do that all the time, even with my own bloody wife. Serena took me back to the world of my youth. For the first time I felt as if someone loved me for who I was.

These days, though, she made me nervous. I wasn't sure what the fuck was going on in her head. It just made me anxious, and I hated feeling that way.

I silenced my phone and looked at Meeru who was applying a fresh coat of pink lipstick. Meeru was safe, she was older, divorced and a mother of two. These were the best kind of women, easy to handle, and they didn't expect anything except a good fuck. They knew exactly what the relationship was all about. But, then again, an older woman couldn't possibly have the kind of vivacity and life that Serena had. My phone rang again—Serena.

'Well, well, Mr Khanna, who's calling you so fervently at this hour? Your wife?' asked Meeru. She had just done a line of Charlie. Her eyes were watery and her nose red.

'Oh, God, no,' I said, shuddering at the thought of Preiti calling me.

'I know her, she's a sweet girl,' said Meeru.

'Excuse me?'

'I know Serena, she's a friend of mine,' she laughed.

'Yeah, Serena is a fun chick,' I said, reaching for the pile of cocaine that was on the table. I took a pinch of the good stuff and rubbed it into my gums. I then lit a cigarette and took a long drag. Amazing. The cocaine had made my gums numb and the smoke from the cigarette felt so damn good.

How the fuck did Meeru know about Serena? I just hoped that Serena hadn't been talking. I wouldn't expect her to, but then again, she was so damn young. What the hell did she know about Delhi and the way shit happened here?

Mumta interrupted my thoughts. '*Madame et monsieur*, we are now off to bed,' she slurred, obviously drunk.

'But feel free to stay here for as long as you please,' added Aveesh, his eyes hazy under his bushy grey eyebrows. He bowed with a flourish and Mumta giggled.

'Thanks, man,' I said. 'Meeru and I are going to finish this game and then we'll leave.' I got up and gave them both a hug.

Meeru and I continued the game in silence, sitting across from each other, both pretending to look intently at the cards though I noticed her peeking at me every now and then. I couldn't blame her. I was wearing just my pink striped boxers and my well-shaped, recently waxed chest was on display. The next time I caught her looking at me, I winked.

Meeru laughed. 'You, my friend, are too sexy for your own good. Is what the other women say correct? Are you a playboy?'

'Well, darling, I guess that is up to you to find out,' I replied.

She looked at me with a serious expression. Aha! I knew that look. This was my chance. I stared back, taking hold of her chin as I slowly inched towards her. I continued to look at her the entire time, straight into her eyes, and I could feel her melt under my stare. I began to kiss her, gently at first, and then more insistently. As expected my fervour began to arouse her. I felt her relax and slowly let go. Instinctively my hand reached for her breasts . . .

Serena's face flashed in front of my eyes. I knew Meeru knew her; women were so sensitive about these things sometimes, I don't know why. I had known Meeru for years, but she had never looked like this. She looked hot. There was no need for Serena to find out. And even if she did, she would understand, and if she didn't understand, she would learn. Everyone slept around in Delhi. Husbands, wives, girlfriends, boyfriends were swapped every season. It wasn't a big deal. She'd understand.

We had been sitting on the cool marble floor, and I now found myself on my back with Meeru on top, touching me in such an amazing way. In a matter of seconds I tore the remaining clothes off her body and thrust into her. I felt myself slowly slipping into the world of sex and drugs.

Afterwards we both lay on the floor, panting. The cold marble felt good against my sweaty skin. A few minutes later I got up and cut a couple of lines. Fuck, I couldn't even think any more. The cocaine and alcohol had just numbed my brain. I lay on my back and stared at the painting on the wall, enjoying the way the colours all merged into one. I couldn't even look at Meeru, she was disgusting. My mind was totally fucked, just a minute ago I was screwing her, and now . . . basically I was fucked. Out of the corner of my eye I saw her get up, gather her clothes and get dressed.

'Amar?' I didn't reply, keeping my eyes shut. She nudged my shoulder with her toe. 'Are you okay?'

'Yeah, baby,' I replied. 'You were amazing. I'm just meditating,' I said slowly, trying not to slur.

'Well, I need to get home, but will you be okay?'

I nodded slowly, 'Oh, yeah, don't worry about me.'

I opened my eyes to see her walking towards the door, holding her heels and handbag. 'Meeru?' I called out.

144

'Yes?'

I wasn't able to talk, but this was important. I had to tell her this. 'Meeru, you have to promise me one thing.'

'What?' she asked a little impatiently.

'Don't tell that friend of yours, okay?' I was passing out.

'What the hell are you talking about, Amar?'

'That dear friend of ours . . . Serena.'

Serena

They were out of town again. They often went away for the weekend these days. Randeep didn't like to stay at home because of me, he couldn't bear to see my face. Being in the same room as me made him unusually angry. After that fight, he hadn't said a word to me, and that was more than a month ago. I wanted to say sorry, but my mom shook her head, 'No, beta, there is no point. Just let him be,' and I complied. It didn't matter much to me anyways, I enjoyed the empty house and being alone.

I remember my fear of sleeping alone for most of my life. Till I was eighteen, when I left India for New York, I had not spent a single night alone. During my first semester at NYU, I was assigned a single room in the dormitory, and every night I would stay awake with every light on, sitting on my extra-long twin bed in my coffin-sized room. Finally when the sun rose and New York City burst into activity, I'd fall into a deep slumber.

After my first midterms when I got Ds in most of my classes I realized I had to do something about this fear. I had always done well at school and my terrible grades worried me a great deal. Painfully I taught myself to fall asleep at night, with every light on, my face covered with a blanket.

The next semester wasn't a problem anyways, I had met Salman by then, and we spent most nights together, either in my dorm room or in his small studio apartment in Murray Hill.

Sometimes I missed him so much. God, we used to be so passionate about each other. It was a stormy, torrid affair, like the roller-coaster ride at the Seven Flags theme park that he had taken me to on our first date—there were so many ups and downs, turns and twists. It was thrilling and exhausting, revitalizing and consuming, all at the same time.

Unexpected tears filled my eyes. I knew that somewhere deep inside, he still loved me, but I also knew that we would never be together again, not after what had happened. Thinking about those dark days I felt my heart pound and a nervous chill go up my spine.

Paneer pasanda—that's where it all started. It was a Saturday night and as usual I cooked him dinner after which we watched a Hindi movie. We had to stop the movie midway because the print of the pirated movie wasn't very clear. Instead we made love, and as we lay intertwined on my pink bedsheet, I casually told him that I hadn't got my period yet. This was a little strange since usually I was regular as clockwork. He was sleepy and content so he gave me a hug and told me to chill.

The next morning I made him his favourite breakfast—pancakes, eggs, bacon and toast. As I was cooking, I saw the remnants of the paneer pasanda on the countertop and a wave of nausea hit me. It was so strong, that I ran to the bathroom and threw up. Salman looked worried from where he sat on the couch. I didn't realize what was happening, but he had figured it out.

We waited a week, and when I still hadn't got my period, he decided that I should take a pregnancy test. I looked at him in worry, but he just squeezed my hand and told me he was being overly cautious. We were always very careful, we always used a condom. The home pregnancy kit was negative, but Salman then insisted I should go to the doctor at the NYU clinic. He dropped me off outside the clinic and waited in the library.

I had been to the clinic before for vaccinations, flu shots and check-ups, and I detested the cold, sterile atmosphere. I peed into the clear plastic container and then handed it over to the nurse in blue. She told me that I would have to wait while they checked the sample, which really annoyed me because I wanted to go home and take a nap. I had been feeling very tired lately. I was sure it was because I was going to get my period. This stupid test Salman insisted on was such a waste of time.

I browsed through boring health magazines for an hour before another robotic, blue-uniformed nurse called my name, 'Serena Sharma? Doctor Britto will see you in room number four. I'll take you there.'

I followed the nurse into a room where a solemn-looking lady sat at a desk browsing through a file. 'Hi, I'm Doctor Britto,' she said. 'We just got the results of your test.' She then cleared her throat and looked down at the paper she was holding.

Her pause made me nervous. She continued in a neutral and flat voice like a cab driver telling me the fare, 'Serena, it's positive.'

I was shocked. Pregnant? It couldn't be. My hand went straight to my tummy, which felt exactly as it always had. 'Doctor, that's just not possible. The test must be incorrect.' I laughed nervously. 'You probably tested someone else's pee.'

Dr Britto didn't laugh or smile. She looked at me seriously through her thick square glasses. 'Serena, you're pregnant, there is no doubt about it.'

I didn't know what to say. I felt nothing and my mind was blank. She waited patiently, till finally I took a deep breath and said with conviction, 'Doctor, something has to be wrong. I . . . I am a responsible individual and we always use condoms, every single time. I just can't be pregnant.' I felt a shiver go down my back, nervousness taking over my body as I looked at Dr Britto's calm and serious face.

'Serena, I'm sorry this came as a surprise to you. It's always unnerving when you are not expecting it. And you know condoms work only ninety-seven per cent of the time. That is why we suggest girls go on the pill as well.'

My head was spinning and I could see spots before my eyes. I wanted to cry, but I was numb. Everything seemed blurry all of a sudden, the doctor's face, the fluorescent lights, the white tiled floor. This was not real, this was just a dream . . . a bad, bad dream.

'Serena, are you all right?'

I looked at the doctor and slowly nodded. She placed a hand on my shoulder. 'Listen, there are people here to help you, okay? Counsellors, nurses, doctors. Please feel free to come here whenever you want.'

I nodded again and slowly stood up and left the room, my life upside down. I was in a daze and before I knew it I was in the car with Salman. All I could think about was the doctor telling me I was pregnant.

Salman didn't say much when I told him. He wasn't shocked or surprised, it was as if he had always known. He just hugged me and held me close.

How could this happen to us? Salman was always so careful, and we always used a condom. Did the condom break without our realizing it? I still wasn't convinced, so I went to the pharmacy and bought three home pregnancy tests. All three were positive. A sense of deep dread crept over me and I felt as if my stomach was hollow. There was no doubt about it. I was pregnant.

The following weeks were extremely difficult. I woke up sick every morning, and for days I couldn't eat anything except raw mangoes. The sight of food made my stomach churn.

Salman and I fought a lot, usually about the abortion. He had suggested the abortion though I knew we couldn't keep the baby. He gently told me my life would change, and I wasn't ready for that yet. I was unnecessarily emotional and had screamed at him and told him he was a selfish jerk, a child killer, how could he not want me to give birth to the baby we had created. He calmly tried to explain to me that a child would mean a great deal of responsibility, emotionally and financially. My life would change, I would have to drop out of college. He would help, of course, but my life as the mother would change far more and that was the sad truth of it. I was livid, I asked him to leave, pushing him out myself when he refused. Before he left he told me calmly that I would have to choose, it was either him or that, he said as he pointed to my stomach. He told me that at this stage of his life he couldn't be responsible for a child. It was too much pressure. The only way for us to remain together was for me to have the abortion.

I knew there was no choice but to go ahead with the abortion, but I was reluctant for some reason. After I calmed down I called him and said I needed some time to think about it.

Over the next few months, we fought every single day. Salman had changed. He blamed me for continuing with the pregnancy and postponing the decision to have an abortion. He avoided seeing me and spending time together. I was so sad, this was the time when I needed him the most. He had never been much of a drinker, but now he regularly went out drinking with his friend Randy, coming home drunk almost every night. He was terrible and insensitive.

One incident is vivid in my memory. I was in the car with Salman and Randy. We were on our way to Salman's dad's birthday party at their house in the Bronx. His mom had cooked spicy curries, biryanis and succulent kababs, which I normally loved, but now the mere thought of all the food made me sick. I pleaded with Salman to take me to the supermarket to buy some fruit. It was all I could stomach these days. He didn't say anything, but drove in the direction of the market. When we got there he turned towards me and said, 'Take five minutes to get whatever you want.'

I had been feeling especially nauseous that day so I asked him sweetly, 'Baby, could you please get me a few raw mangoes? I'm not feeling well.'

'Serena, we don't have a lot of time. Just go and get it, okay?' he said in an annoyed tone.

In the rear-view mirror I saw Randy smirking. How dare Salman treat me like this in front of him? What would Randy think of me? What kind of weak girl was I to take this kind of shit from the man whose baby I was carrying?

'Salman, I'm really not up to it, could you go?' I said more assertively.

He turned on the ignition and the car began to purr. 'Serena, I am leaving in two minutes. If you don't come back by then, I'll go without you.'

Rage shot through my body and I looked at him with eyes burning with fury. How could he speak to me like this? In my anger I reached towards the door. Suddenly, I felt a sharp, tingling pain against my face. It took me a few seconds to realize that Salman had slapped me.

He looked me square in the face. 'Don't you dare behave with me this way, you understand?'

I was breathing heavily now, my chest heaving. 'Fuck you,' I said as I stepped out of the car and walked away. I expected him to come after me to apologize for his despicable behaviour, but he didn't. When I turned around, I saw his blue Honda drive away.

I cried for an entire hour while I sat at a nearby coffee shop and then took a cab to his house. When I got there, his mother hugged me and with concern in her eyes asked me what was wrong. Why were we always fighting nowadays? I shook my head, tears streaming down my face. 'Nothing, Aunty, nothing at all,' I sobbed. 'It was just a silly fight.' What else could I possibly tell her?

By now all our close friends knew—Randy, my best friend Jasleen, Salman's sister Sameera. They were all on his side, even Jasleen. They thought an abortion was the only option. Couldn't they see the way he treated me? Were they blind? The only one who was kind and sympathetic towards me was Raja, Sameera's fiancé. He believed that I should have the right to decide whether I wanted to keep the baby or not. He once even yelled at Sameera when she told me that I had to take 'it' out of my body.

But I was worried about Salman the most. I barely saw him any more. The more time I spent at home, the more he stayed away. Between work and his drinking sessions with Randy he didn't have any time for me.

I went to the Upper West side for my twenty-week sonogram because it was cheaper than anywhere downtown. The minute I got there, I liked the place. My doctor's name was Shakira, a loud, exuberant African American woman with long braids. She was funny and friendly and made the unpleasant procedure somewhat bearable.

Shakira didn't know that I was contemplating having an abortion and I didn't have the heart to tell her. How could I tell this lovely woman, who told me she was the mother of five children, that I might kill my baby?

She had asked me if wanted to know the sex of the child, and I just couldn't resist. As I sat there with Shakira I felt as if I was in a different world, one where abortions did not exist, where I would be the proud mother of a beautiful baby girl.

Before I left I took the pashmina stole I was wearing and draped it around Shakira's neck.

'How soft!' she said, laughing.

'It's for you,' I told her.

'No, hon, I can't take this from you.'

I took her hand in mine, 'Shakira, if you don't accept this, I will feel terrible. Consider it a small token of thanks . . . from us,' I added, placing my hand on my tummy.

As I left Shakira's clinic I realized I had to take a decision about the abortion. I had put it off for too long. I now knew I was carrying a girl and as I thought about the kind of life I'd be able to provide my child, I knew I didn't have a choice. I was a single woman, a student. I couldn't afford to raise a child alone. I knew Salman wouldn't marry me if I kept this baby. He had made that very clear. And I couldn't go back to India as an unwed mother—what would my family say? What about Papa's reputation as a senior police officer? When I reached home I informed Salman of my decision. He was thrilled and wasted no time in setting up an appointment.

The next day I sat in the cold NYU clinic with stainless steel desks, white plastic chairs, tiled floors and grim-looking nurses walking around purposefully in blue uniforms. I couldn't bear to look at the patients. I was sure everyone there knew what I was going to do, the guilt evident on my face. Salman and I waited in silence, staring at the large colourful posters on the walls.

I leaned against Salman's warm body and he squeezed my trembling hand reassuringly. A nurse took us to a examining room, where a doctor conducted a sonogram. She was young and very pretty and as soon as she smiled I was at ease. She talked and laughed a lot, asking us where we were from and what we did. She told us she loved India. She had gone there while in college and had visited Delhi, Mumbai, Bangalore, and, of course, Goa, which was her favourite.

Under normal circumstances I love chatting with random people, but that day I had no desire to speak to anyone. I stayed quiet, smiling politely every now and then. Salman answered most of the questions she asked like when did we first find out, what method of birth control we used, was I on any medication, did I have any medical problems.

I would have answered the questions myself, but I was afraid I would start crying if I spoke.

In the end she told us we had waited too long. We definitely couldn't use abortion pills and it was now very risky to even operate. Very few doctors would take the chance and abort now as the foetus was quite developed.

I started crying. I knew I couldn't keep this baby. What had made me postpone the decision for so long? The doctor gave me a hug, gently patting my back, and told me that it would be okay. I would learn to take care of the child and would make a great mother. She gave me her cellphone number and told me to call her if I needed anything.

Salman was livid when we left the clinic. I knew he blamed me for this situation. As soon as he dropped me off at his apartment, he disappeared. He didn't return till late at night when he told me he had found a doctor who was willing to go ahead with the abortion. I was scared, but I knew this was the best option and so I agreed.

This doctor wasn't as nice as any of the previous ones I had met. He was cold and looked kind of cruel. When I confessed this to Salman he told me to stop reacting stupidly and to rein in my wild imagination. The abortion was scheduled for the next day at the doctor's clinic, which was dingy and dirty.

I woke up to Salman's worried face. There were bright lights hurting my eyes. It was then that I felt the pain, greater than any I had ever experienced. It was so intense that I thought I was dying. I had broken my leg years ago and I could remember the horror of that pain, but this was something else. This pain made me want to give up my life.

I then noticed the bloody sheets and plastic gloves. I immediately began retching and soon after that I fainted. When I gained consciousness I was in a light, airy hospital room. Salman was holding a bouquet of daisies, my favourite flowers, as he spoke to a nurse. He turned to me as she left and explained what had happened. The doctor had botched my abortion and had left me bleeding on the operating table. Salman had found me in that state and rushed me to the emergency room. I could go home now but I had to take it easy for a few weeks.

Jasleen, Sameera and Raja were waiting for me at home with flowers and a cake. Jasleen had made aloo gobi just the way I like it—spicy with Punjabi masalas. After everyone had left I lay in bed with Salman's arms wrapped around me.

Two days later I woke up bleeding and I was burning up with fever. The doctor told me that I had caught an infection and that I would bleed for a while.

I was miserable. Night after night I lay awake, thoughts of the abortion flooding my mind. I dreamt of the beautiful child that I had killed—a beautiful, healthy baby girl. I saw Salman holding her in his arms, smiling, laughing, the three of us in Central Park, a small happy family. While Salman slept on the couch, I cried myself to sleep almost every night. The guilt of having taken the life of my own child gave me nightmares.

The abortion changed me as a person and it changed my relationship with Salman. We didn't fight any more, but that was because I hardly ever saw him. When he was at home we didn't speak much, he didn't hold me, he didn't even look me in the eye. This painful, uncomfortable silence was far worse than the fighting. I could see him drift away from me, and the closer I tried to get to him, the farther he pushed me away.

The worst part was that he was normal around other people, in fact he was better than normal. In the past we never had people over, now he entertained almost every night. His friends would come over, drink, rummage through my kitchen for snacks and while they had a good time, I lay alone in my bedroom. Sometimes Salman asked me to cook for them, and I did it thinking it would somehow make him love me again, but after his friends left he was back to being cold, silent and distant. No matter what I did, it was never enough. And the fact that I couldn't have sex didn't make things any easier. It was as if my body was punishing me for the crime that I had committed against it.

It was a beautiful day when Salman asked me to marry him. It was a while after the abortion, just as my life was getting back to normal. He was unusually nice to me that day. I was in bed eating Chinese food when he came home from work. He hugged me and gave me a long, deep kiss. He then asked me out for dinner and said he wanted to make it a special evening. We went to our favourite restaurant, Sammy's, on the South Street Seaport. It wasn't very fancy, but it had the best lobster in town and we only went there on special occasions.

When I asked him what was happening he just kissed me and told me I looked pretty.

I was really surprised to see Salman wearing a tie and I jokingly pulled at it and ran my fingers through his neatly combed hair. I wished I looked nicer. Looking at my uneven, chipped nails I realized I should have done them. I hadn't dressed up for such a long time that I had almost forgotten how to.

We sat at a quiet candlelit table in a corner. This too was strange since we usually sat at the bar or at a table in front where the service was quicker. Salman insisted that we order a bottle of wine. I chose the cheapest bottle on the menu because I knew Salman and I would split the bill like we always did and I didn't have any savings left since after the abortion.

That evening was so romantic, it reminded me of the past when we were madly in love. Salman was a true gentleman, he held my hand through the night and occasionally reached across the table to stroke my hair. We even kissed more than we usually did. After we had ordered dessert he took my hand in his and with a serious look on his face said he needed to discuss something with me. A feeling of dread shot through my body. I knew this was all too good to be true. I was convinced he was breaking up with me. He told me tenderly that he loved me and that he knew I loved him. He said we both knew we wanted to get married and since it was going to happen sooner or later, it might as well be now. He told me he knew he had been acting difficult lately, and that I was sad. He believed the engagement would help us. It would do him good to have a beautiful, loving girl by his side.

He then got down on one knee, took out a ring and asked me to marry him. I was so stunned and happy and delighted that I was totally at a loss for words, and that did not happen often. I simply nodded and then pulled him towards me and kissed him.

Seconds later, a waiter came with a bouquet of red roses and a big chocolate cake and everyone in the restaurant cheered. I slid the ring on to my finger and continued to stare at it the entire night. It was totally perfect, a solitaire with a platinum band and it felt perfect on my finger. I kept it on all the time, in the shower, when I went to bed, while washing dishes. I finally took it off the day we broke up and threw it into the stormy grey Hudson where it landed without the slightest ripple.

After Salman proposed I thought it was the end of all the fighting, bitterness and pain. But I was wrong—it just got worse. We both tried to make it work, pretending as if nothing was wrong, but things just weren't the same any more. Somehow every fight would end with him storming out after I had accused him of killing my baby. I tried not to bring it up, I really did, but I couldn't understand why he would propose after he made me abort our child.

Seeing how bad things were between Salman and me, Jasleen invited me to spend the weekend at her parents' house in Jersey. She thought it would do me good to spend a few days away from him and I agreed. It would give us both the space and time apart that we so badly needed. I was glad to get away from the city and from Salman.

At Jasleen's home, I felt the thoughts of the abortion slowly slipping away for the first time in months. It was lovely being a kid again, forgetting about my life and responsibilities in New York. Like teenagers we spent the weekend splashing around in the pool, browsing through fashion magazines, watching movies and feasting on her mom's cooking.

The bitter feelings I had felt for Salman over the
past few months seemed to dissipate and I found
myself thinking fondly of him. When I ate the
yummy butter chicken that Jasleen's mom cooked,
I thought of making it for him. After an especially
good movie I thought of how we would have
enjoyed it together. I wondered if he also thought
about me all the time.

When I mentioned this to Jasleen she told me to
forget about him. 'Let this weekend be ours,' she
said giving me a hug. But how could I forget about
him? After all I loved him, he was the man whose
baby I had carried. I realized that I wanted nothing
more than for us to be like we were before all the
crap—absolutely, totally crazy about each other.

On Sunday morning I said goodbye to Jasleen
and her parents and boarded the New Jersey Transit
back to the City, with butter chicken in tow for
Salman. I was meant to return on Monday, but I
missed him and wanted to get back quickly. On the
ride home I felt calm, peaceful and happy. I hadn't
felt this way for a long while. I had finally stopped
bleeding this weekend and I longed to be with him
again. From the Port Authority station I walked to
our apartment in Murray Hill. I was sure Salman

would be home. He loved ordering Indian food and watching football on Sunday afternoons.

I walked up the creaky stairs to our third-floor apartment and smiled fondly at the door where I had placed a small Ganesha idol just like the one we had at our home in Chandigarh. I opened the door to the apartment and was disappointed to find it quiet—no TV, no Salman. I wanted to see him so much. I walked into the kitchen to put the butter chicken in the fridge and suddenly I got the feeling that the apartment wasn't empty. I noticed that the door to our bedroom was closed, which was strange because we never shut that door. I walked to the door, twisted the doorknob and opened it. I found them on my pink bedsheet, wrapped around each other, Salman's arm slung loosely over her waist, his palm resting near her navel, exactly the way he held me. They stared back at me with blank, groggy expressions.

I turned around and walked out of the apartment. It was October, my favourite month in New York. I was warm in my fleece jacket and so I went for a long walk in Central Park, the cool breeze blowing through my hair, turning the tip of my nose pale pink. The perfectly blue sky was dotted with billowy white clouds and the sun shone down on me. I found a spot where the sun was strong and stood there basking for a few moments, taking in the bustling, noisy city that I loved and hated at the same time. People marched about in fall colours, brown, grey, khaki. The wind whistled, brown leaves fell to the pavement. I thought of how my life would have been if I had had the baby. Salman and I would have lived in New York. I would have been a mother, a wife, a daughter-in-law, waking up early in the morning, cooking meals, changing diapers. A tear rolled down my cheek as I mourned for what could have been.

Today is Papa's birthday. I woke up with puffy eyes, the mascara from the night before forming dark circles under them. In another life I would have woken up early on this day and run into my parents' room, jumping into their big bed with the card I had made for Papa and the shiny balloons I had bought with the money I had saved up. Papa would have groaned on being woken up so early and would have enveloped me in a bear hug.

Birthdays were always special for him. He'd take the day off and we'd spend it together. I remember one special birthday when we were in London. We had lunch at Covent Garden and then walked through Hyde Park. Papa bought presents for us as well—a ring for Mama and the latest Barbie doll for me. We had a big party in the evening. I was supposed to be in bed, but I snuck out in my pyjamas and looked at the distinguished men in suits and the women in dazzling saris in awe. I gazed proudly at my parents, the most handsome couple in the room, standing side by side, totally in love with each other.

I went to the gurdwara and prayed for Papa's happiness in heaven. I thanked him for the wonderful life he had given me and told him that he was the best father a girl could ever have. I found a certain peace by sitting in the corner of the small quiet gurdwara, lost in my thoughts, letting my mind wander. If Papa were alive today, he would be sad at the way I had turned out. I had tried so hard to make him a happy and proud father, and I had succeeded for a while. He was so excited about my admission to NYU and my decision to go to America all by myself. But then all the crap had started and I just couldn't deal with it. Everything happened so fast, like falling dominoes, one terrible thing after another. The break-up with Salman followed by Papa's death had made me suicidal. It seemed easier to just stop than to pick myself up and start again. But I did manage to brush the grime and dirt off and limp onwards, though I had no clue where I was going. This wasn't the life Papa had wanted for me, but at least it was a life and in some small way it made me happy.

The phone rang at 3 a.m. I didn't want to see him, especially today. I didn't pick up the phone. I knew I wouldn't be able to say no if I did, I never could. But he called again and again until I was fed up and finally answered.

'Hey sexy, how are ya?' he said.

'I'm good, Amar. You?'

'Can I see you right now?' he slurred.

'I don't think so. I'm not in town.' I felt bad about lying to him, but he was so insistent otherwise.

'But I'm dying to see you, baby.'

'Amar, I told you I'm not in Delhi, I'm in Chandigarh.'

'I know, but I really want to see you.' He was totally fucked, I could tell by the way he was speaking.

'Babe, you're high,' I said. 'I can't see you right now because I'm not in Delhi.' I tried sounding as stern as possible.

'Well, I'm going to come to you then.'

'Right now?'

'Yes, this very second.' I laughed because I knew he was in no position to drive to Chandigarh. He would probably pass out in the next two minutes. 'Okay, hotness, I'll see you soon. I'll call you when I get there,' he said.

I hung up the phone and slowly unclenched my fist. Amar's phone calls made me so nervous and anxious. It took so much out of me to just say no to him. I wanted him so badly that it was scary. I felt like picking up the phone this very second and asking him to meet me. I hated the fact that I couldn't run into his arms whenever I wanted to, I couldn't see him when my heart desired. I could only see him when he called me. I understood the situation. He'd explained it to me a thousand times, but that didn't stop me from hating it.

Maybe, one day, we would run away together to some place far away where no one knew Amar Khanna or Serena Sharma. We would leave this

life, this country, these memories, far, far behind.
We would roam the streets hand in hand like any
other happy couple. We would do as we pleased,
and we wouldn't have to care about who saw us
or who knew us. We would be like a real couple,
the way Salman and I had been. We would live
together, raise a family and face the trials and
tribulations of life as one.

I wanted what I never had with Salman. I was
still in love with him. On days when I felt low
and terrible, like today, I thought of him and he
lifted my spirits. I closed my eyes and I thought
of him holding me, caressing my hair, and I felt a
warm glow inside. But I loved Amar too. I would
throw away everything—my life, my family—to
be with him. I would be a mother to his son. I
would treat his child like I would have treated my
daughter. But the uncertainty of our relationship
was agonizing. I never knew when I would see him
next. My biggest fear was that he would go away
and never come back. I didn't know if I would
hear from him tomorrow or the day after. I didn't
know if he would answer the phone when I called
him. I didn't know if there would be a next time,

but despite everything, I yearned for our stolen moments together and cherished every second with him because that time was ours and no one could take that away from me.

Riya

I was in the midst of a heated argument with my father when I got a phone call. It was Serena's mother. I wondered why she was calling me. What nefarious activity was Serena up to this time? I didn't want to take the call, but I figured it would be rude.

'Namaste, Aunty, how are you?'

'Riya,' she sobbed, 'she's dead.'

'What?' I said, thinking I must have heard wrong.

She continued, her voice quivering 'Yes, beta, she's dead. The funeral is at three. Do come if you can.'

My head spun, round and round. I could see black and red spots before my eyes and I felt as if my head would burst at any moment because it was filled with so much chaos. I lay down. I don't remember when the dizziness stopped, but I lay there for many hours thinking that this couldn't possibly be true. It had to be a bad dream. I was going to wake up any second now and find myself arguing with my father.

Her mother didn't tell me how she died or when, and I didn't ask. I wanted to call someone, anyone, who knew us both. I found Vik's card and called him. 'Dude, this is so fucking crazy, it's not even funny. I'm totally shattered,' he said.

'Yeah,' I agreed, 'I just can't believe it. Do you know what exactly happened? Her mom called me, and I didn't want to ask her.'

'Yeah, dude, so fucked up. I don't have the details, but Amar and she were doing some shit that was laced and all that usual bull. They're trying to figure it out.'

'Okay, Vik, thanks. I'll talk to you later,' I said.

'Yeah, babe, you're okay, right? I know you and Serena were tight and all.'

'I'm fine, Vik. Just a little shocked,' I replied.

'I know what you mean. All of us are pretty shattered too. It's a lot to handle.'

'Thanks, Vik. I'll see you later.'

'Yeah, no problem. This is so fucking crazy. See ya, babe.'

I hung up the phone feeling numb. I felt as if I had been punched in the stomach and was waiting for the terrible pain to set in.

Three days before Diwali, on Wednesday, 20 October, at 7.32 a.m., Amar Khanna and Serena Sharma were found dead in a penthouse apartment in Gurgaon. They were doing cocaine which was laced with other chemicals. Both died within hours of consumption. The cleaner found their naked bodies in the bathtub. There was cocaine everywhere—on the floor, on their bodies, in her vagina.

For the next few days the press was all over the story. Serena had always yearned to be photographed and written about. In the end at least one of her dreams came true. She was on the front page of every newspaper. The media discussed drug trafficking in Delhi, the boisterous partying ways of the younger generation. Religious fundamentalists and the moral police were up in arms. Nightclubs were shut down, liquor licences suspended. This happened every year in Delhi. A famous person—socialite, film star or politician—died from an overdose and the Delhi police would clamp down on the city's nightlife. For a short while, parties would come to a standstill and drugs would be hard to source, but a few weeks later, things would be back to normal, until someone else died and the cycle would begin anew.

I should have attended her funeral, but I just didn't have the guts. I did go and visit her mother a few weeks later. She was glad to see me. She said the funeral had turned into a comic show. Much to her mother's regret most of Delhi's socialites turned up wearing Gucci sunglasses, their heads wrapped in Hermès scarves.

Parmeet Aunty showed me photographs of Serena as a happy, chubby child, a young girl in her blue-and-white school uniform with two lopsided ponytails, with her mother, stepfather and baby sister, just like I remembered her—blonde hair, blue eyeshadow, bright smile. She also showed me a photograph that the police had taken of her body. She had kept it for some morbid reason, and I couldn't understand why she showed it to me. There she was, her naked body lying next to Amar's, grey in death. They were on their sides, their limbs were intertwined, a pool of blood between them at the bottom of the tub. Her blonde hair and the red blood added bright colour to the stark yellow and grey photograph.

Sitaram

I slowly took the sachet out of my pocket and slipped the powder into the ice tray. Overnight the water would crystallize into ice and tomorrow I would use the ice cubes for the drink that Sahib had every evening. Tiny beads of sweat broke out on my forehead even though it was cold in the old kitchen. My hands shook as I emptied the plastic pouch of its white contents.

I chanted the Lord's name in my mind, again and again, trying to rid myself of the sin. I needed the money. That was the only reason why I was doing it. The growing tumour in my stomach, my wife's pregnancy and my mother's illness had drained my savings. I touched the crisp notes in my pocket with pleasure and thought about the ease it would provide.

I saw the white grains dissolve in the water and with a trembling hand placed the tray in the freezer.

Just one more step and I would be a rich man.

It was a cold winter night and despite the three sweaters and the thick, scratchy woollen blanket I shivered. The cold seemed to rise up from the floor through the thin mattress. I could think of nothing else but those white grains in the plastic pouch and what they would do to Sahib. I told myself I shouldn't care about anything, after all I was just an instrument, a tool, a middleman. I was born a poor man, and I was just doing what I could to earn a fair living. I started shivering uncontrollably and touched the notes that lay under the wispy pillow for solace.

Six days ago, on a lazy winter morning in Chandigarh, I was taking a mid-morning snooze on my favourite spot on the carpet in the living room. The telephone had woken me and for a second I contemplated letting it ring, but then I feared it may be Sahib, so I painfully got up, my arthritic knee creaking. I instantly recognized the voice on the other end. It was Memsahib, who had abandoned me, leaving me all alone with the grumpy Sahib.

'Sitaram, everything okay?' she asked in her melodic voice.

THE GREAT INDIAN LOVE STORY

'Memsahib, by your grace, all is well,' I said, unable to conceal my excitement.

'Sitaram, I need to meet you, I am sending a car to pick you up at four o'clock.'

'Yes, Memsahib, of course.'

I wondered what she could possibly want from me. Fear slowly crept over me. Did she miss that ring I had stealthily placed in my pocket two years ago? Had she realized that fruits and vegetables were cheaper than what I had told her? Despite the fear I was excited to see her. She was so beautiful, prettier than any actress. I used to spy on her through the cracked window pane as she bathed. That fair, fleshy bosom, her long curly hair—the thought of her awakened something inside me.

The car took me to a small hotel on the outskirts of the city. The driver led me to a room where she sat in a chair waiting for me. She looked as lovely as ever, and as I bent to touch her feet, I sneaked a look at her low neckline.

She was so kind to me, offering me tea. She had inquired about my wife and mother before moving on to business. She extracted a pouch from her purse and told me I needed to administer this to Sahib, surreptitiously through his drink, and for my efforts I would be rewarded generously. She took out a bundle of crisp notes, held together by an orange rubber band, and handed it to me. She promised me I would get another bundle once the deed was done.

How could I have said no? After all, she was my beautiful, beloved Memsahib. She had given me everything I ever needed. She had taught me how to cook, lent me money for my sister's wedding and for my father's operation. This was just a small, tiny favour, a way to repay her for all she had done for me. Of course, the money helped.

Before I left I asked her if I would get into trouble. She had laughed away my fears and told me not to worry.

I followed her strict instructions and filled the silver ice bucket with the neatly formed square cubes, placing it on the tray along with the bottle of whisky. I slowly made my way up the stairs to Sahib's room. My hands were trembling so much that I almost dropped the tray. I struggled to open the whisky bottle and Sahib cursed me and shooed me away with a dirty look.

As usual I went to bed before Sahib, but I was unable to sleep. A chilling feeling of guilt slowly snuck up my spine. I thought of the white grains dissolving in the water and my Memsahib's beautiful, fair face. I don't know when I fell asleep, but I was woken up early the next morning by Serena's piercing shrieks.

Epilogue

Serena's death jolted me out of my stupor. I realized that I couldn't let my life just pass me by. I was a dreamer and I usually let things take their own course, drifting along wherever life took me. Serena was a victim of aimlessness. She lost control of her life, letting the city take over her fragile mind and body. I couldn't let that happen to me.

I did not want to return to America any more. That life seemed to belong to the past. There wasn't much left for me there any more. Through Serena I had discovered a little bit of what India had become since I had left many years ago and now I was curious to know more. Serena was not strong enough to make it here, but I wanted to, for her sake. I wanted to build a life for myself and have friends. They didn't have to own big farmhouses or throw fancy parties. They just had to be real.

I studied for hours on end for entrance exams and I surprised myself and my family by getting into the Indian Institute of Management in Bangalore. I visited the school and I really liked it. The campus was green and peaceful and there was a focussed energy about the place.

And so, just like that, I began a new life in India. Now, a year later, I have blurry memories of those nights with Serena—the alcohol and cocaine, the palatial farmhouses and glitzy parties. It was all fun while it lasted, a bit surreal really, and I haven't seen that side of Delhi since. I doubt I ever will. Now when I come back to Delhi during vacations and drive past imposing black gates and high walls, I wonder if this was one of the homes where I had partied during my crazy nights with Serena. Whenever I go to Soul, I always think of her—voluptuous and curvy with blonde hair, standing in front of the mirror in bright red panties with a black bow.

Serena has touched and shaped my life in ways that I still can't fully understand. It would not be truthful to say I miss her deeply, but I do find myself thinking of her and her colourful stories. Parmeet Aunty had told me about Serena's past—her failed relationship with Salman and her abortion. I guess there was a lot about her that I did not know. Perhaps I was too quick to judge her. She lived a tragic life, one filled with pain and abandonment, and that was probably the reason for her wild lifestyle.

Serena ended the life of her unborn child out of love for Salman and she destroyed their relationship in the bargain. Parmeet Aunty destroyed Serena's life when she married Randeep, and Serena blamed her for her father's death, saying he died of a broken heart. Devastated by all the loss, Serena destroyed what was left of her life over Amar, a relationship that was doomed from the start. Serena and Parmeet Aunty both fought for love and in the end paid a heavy price for it. In Serena's case, she paid with her life.

I guess I've learnt that selfish, excessive love is corrosive and can shatter lives, but then that doesn't explain the joy in Parmeet Aunty's and Randeep's life or their love for Tanya. Perhaps the truth is that love is indescribable and complex, and we can do nothing except navigate it the best we can.

Author's Note

I'm not going to pretend to be a guru on love, in fact I wish dearly that there was such a guru, but unfortunately all I have is my heart, and my mind that often battles against it. I fell in love for the first time, and it was the most painful, consuming, heart-wrenching experience. I have had boyfriends before, and I liked them all, but none of them could even hold a candle to him. All that soppy stuff about love being blind and irrational—it is true. I pride myself on being a creature of strategy, rationale and self-control, yet I found myself behaving in the most irrational ways, my emotions going berserk, my heart dancing wildly to the tune of a frenzied orchestra, my hormones on speed. It was completely crazy and totally amazing.

I was never able to be with him, but I learnt to celebrate my love in my heart. I learnt to derive joy by just loving him, by feeling myself consumed by a love which transcended everything. The experience was scarring, a scar for which the only healer is time. Yet despite the pain I would never wish for things to be different because I learnt about love. I learnt about what it was like to let my mind, body and heart be consumed, to love another person so much that I would throw away my entire life for that passion. Zeus, you are my love story, because without ever even knowing it you taught me about love. I love you.

Ira